C0-CZY-064

The Reno Kid

"The Beginning"

Copyright © 2011 Allen Russell

ISBN 978-1-61434-508-4

All rights reserved. No part of this publication may be reproduced, stored in a retrieval system, or transmitted in any form or by any means, electronic, mechanical, recording or otherwise, without the prior written permission of the author.

A Reno Kid Book

Published in the United States by The Reno Kid Publishing Group, Reno, NV, a division of Rodeo Bull TV, L.L.C.

The characters and events in this book are fictitious. Any similarity to real persons, living or dead, is coincidental and not intended by the author.

Novel based on the character "The Reno Kid" created by Tom Brooks and Richard Grome
Edited by The Reno Kid Publishing Group.
Cover design by Heritage Group, L.L.C. and The Reno Kid Publishing Group.

Printed in the United States of America on acid-free paper.

Booklocker.com, Inc.
2011

First Edition

The Reno Kid

"The Beginning"

By

Allen Russell

Based on the Reno Kid character created by

Tom Brooks

and

Richard Grome

Contents

Chapter One: Riders of the Dires

"I'm sorry, Son," the doctor said as he emerged from the darkened room. "She hasn't much time...she wants to see you."

"Come closer, Augie," the woman whispered when the boy entered the room. Lying on the small bed with only an oil lamp for light, she looked pale and feeble. Her room was a small windowless space in the basement of the National House Hotel, St. Louis, Missouri.

Young Augustus Alcazar was doing his best to hide his pain as he walked to her side and took her hand, "How are you feeling, Ma?"

"I'm not long for this world."

"No Ma, no...you'll be all right, just wait and see."

"No, Augustus, my life is over and it's time for you to grow up. . . ." A racking cough interrupted her as she fought for another breath, "There isn't...much time." Pausing, she wiped her lip with a blood-stained rag, "you...you listen and listen close."

"I'm listening," he said, as a tear started down his cheek.

"I want you to get away from this place. Civilization killed your father, now it's killed me. The foul air of this city will be your death if you remain here."

"But, where can I go? How will I get there?"

"I know you don't remember much about your father, but he was born of a people who lived many miles to the southwest. His grandfather used to tell him stories of far away and long ago. Your people were kings before the Spanish came and enslaved them. Your father wanted to return to the land of his ancestors, but he died before we could find a way. The blood of kings flows within you, Augustus, always remember that, your destiny is in their land.

"But, I have no way of going anywhere."

"Over there," she said, pointing to the dresser in the corner. "The top drawer, I've been saving it for you." Opening the drawer, Augustus spied a small tin box. Inside, he found several bills and some coins.

"How much is in here?" he asked.

"Seventeen dollars and sixty-seven cents, I know...it isn't much, but. . . ."

1

"It's a lot of money, but how. . . ."

"A few cents every month, for years…the medallion, is it there?"

"Is this it?" Augustus asked, holding up the rustic metal object. The ancient amulet appeared to be made of hammered gold and resembled a man with catlike features.

"A symbol of your ancestors," his mother said, "Put it around your neck…keep it close to. . . ." Before she could finish, another racking cough shook her body. Then, as suddenly as it began, the spasms ceased and she fell silent.

Ma!...Ma!"

"She's gone," the doctor said, pulling the quilt up over the woman's face. "I know you don't understand, but she's better off. The consumption was just too much for her. There was nothing more anyone could do." The doctor removed a small notepad from his bag and scribbled: Marie Alcazar, time of death, 10:30 am, April 30, 1837. "Do you have any family in St. Louis?" he asked the boy when he was finished.

"I don't have family anywhere," Augustus replied.

"Well, don't worry. I'll have someone come for her body."

"Will she go to the potter's field?"

"No," the doctor said, "I'll make arrangements for her to be buried in a decent place."

"I don't have much money."

"I'll take care of the money," Thomas Swain said, entering the room. Swain was the owner of the hotel. "I'm truly sorry for your loss," he added, putting his arm around Augustus' shoulders. "Boy, you can stay here and continue working if you want. I can't pay you as much as I did your mother, but you'd have a roof over your head and something to eat."

"Thank you sir, but her dying wish was for me to get away from this city."

"How old are you, thirteen…fourteen?" Swain asked, "How far do you think you'll get?"

"I don't know, but I'm going to find out."

The next day, a cold rain pelted Augustus' head as he stood by and watched his mother's plain wooden casket being lowered into the ground. Aside from the grave-diggers, the only other person there was Thomas Swain. "Thank you again, sir," Augustus said when the grave was filled in. "This is a nice place."

"It was the least I could do for her," Swain said, "Won't you change your mind about leaving?"

Everything Augustus owned in the world was stuffed in a small rucksack hanging over his shoulder. "No sir, Ma wanted me to go, and I'm going."

Reaching in his pocket, Swain removed a gold coin and handed it to Augustus, "Here's twenty dollars," he said, "Good luck to you."

A twenty-dollar gold-piece was more money than Augustus had ever seen. "I don't...I can't. . . ."

"Take it," Swain said, folding the boy's wet fingers tightly over the coin. When you find fame and fortune, you can pay me back. So long, Augie, take care of yourself, and remember, you'll always have a home here if you want it." As Augustus watched his only friend in the world walk away, he almost went after Swain. Remembering his mother's last words, the boy reluctantly turned and walked into the gloom.

Darkness found Augustus aimlessly wandering the crowded streets of St. Louis. Never before had he felt so alone. He was near the docks at the confluence of the Mississippi and the Missouri Rivers. Since the return of Lewis and Clark in 1806, St. Louis had become the main gateway to the vast unclaimed land simply known to most as, "The West".

Hardly a month would go by without some adventure seeking expedition setting off, up the Missouri River. St. Louis was also the gathering place for hardy and sometimes foolhardy pioneers to head west with their long lines of covered wagons.

Unlike those well financed explorers, Augustus was hungry and tired but reluctant to spend any of his precious money. Passing the door to one of the local saloons, he noticed a crudely lettered handbill.

BOUND FOR CALIFORNIA
THE AMERICAN FUR COMPANY

SEEKS ABLE-BODIED MEN OF SUBSTANCE
SOLDIERS, TRAPPERS, HUNTERS, EXPLORERS
APPLY INSIDE

Augustus went in the door and began surveying the room until he spotted three men sitting at a round table. In addition to the glowing oil lamp, there was a half-empty bottle of whiskey and several glasses. He noticed an opened ledger with several names written in it. Figuring they must be the men he was looking for, Augustus walked over to them.

"What can I do for you, Boy?" one of them asked. He was a smaller man who seemed to be in charge.

"I want to go to California."

"You mean with us?" the man asked, as the other men at the table began to chuckle.

"With the fur company, yes sir."

"This ain't gonna be no church picnic, Sonny."

"I'm not looking for a picnic, church or otherwise," Augustus said, "and I'm bound for the west, alone or with the fur company, matters little to me."

"Well, you got a mouth on you," the man said. "You got a horse or a gun, or are you planning to walk to California? I would wager you don't even own a knife."

"The sign says you're looking for men of substance," Augustus said, "Is that true or not?"

"True enough," the man said, "But, you best get on back to your momma."

"My mother's dead, I put her in the ground this morning."

"Well, I'm sorry about that, but we can't use you."

"Hold on there," another man at the table said. Leaning forward, he put his elbows on the table and stared at Augustus for what seemed like a long time. He was a large dark-skinned man with wild bushy hair and a deep baritone voice, "How old are you, Kid?" he finally asked.

"Going on nineteen," Augustus replied.

"I'd say nearer to fourteen. You got any qualities other than your inclination to lying?"

"I'm a pretty fair cook, my mother taught me."

"You ever packed a mule, rode a horse, trapped beaver, or fought Indians."

"Yes sir," Augustus replied.

"Which one?" the big man asked.

"All of that...and more."

"Another lie, I suspect."

"All right, Boy," the small man said, "We've heard enough, you run along. . . ."

"Are you scared of the dark?" the big man asked.

"No, nor anything else," Augustus replied.

"How 'bout grizzlies and blood-thirsty Indians?"

"Least of all grizzlies and blood-thirsty Indians."

"Sign him up," the big man said, slapping the table, "This kid's an epic liar, but he damn sure ain't timid."

"This boy will never make it to the mountains," the smaller man said.

"I dare say, he'll match you stride for stride," the big man said.

"The company ain't gonna like. . . ."

"Be here at daylight in the morning," the big man said to Augustus. "I like you, Kid. You're entertaining as hell and you got gumption. You remind me of...well...me!"

"I'll be here...yes sir...thank you, Mr...."

"Beckwourth," the big man said, sticking out his hand, "Jim Beckwourth."

Weeks flew by as the fur traders moved steadily west. Under Beckwourth's close watch, Augustus quickly became a skilled horseman. Beckwourth taught him to hit a mark with a Hawken and reload in a hurry. Augustus was eager to learn and the mountain man freely shared his knowledge of life in the wilderness.

Augustus never shirked his responsibilities or complained about anything. He cheerfully did his share and often a little more. The men of the expedition grew to respect him. They were well pleased with the boy's prowess with stewpot and skillet. His mother had indeed taught him well. Buffalo, beaver, or porcupine; the boy could turn practically anything into a good meal.

"Well Kid, what do you think of 'em?" Beckwourth asked his young companion one bright morning.

"Are those the Rockies?" Augustus asked.

They were a month out of St. Louis and sitting horseback, surveying the snow-covered mountain range still two days distant. "The very same," Beckwourth said. "There's no place on earth like 'em, I reckon."

"How long will it be till we get across and on to California?"

"A spell," Beckwourth said. "The Rockies aren't just one range of mountains. When we get across those in front of us, there'll be another and still another. It'll take a couple of months to get to the desert, and then we'll still have the Sierra's to cross before we reach California."

"How is it you know so much about the wilderness?" Augustus asked, "How do you find your way out here?"

"Well, I'll tell you, Kid, I been most everywhere and done most everything. I'm a child of the Crow Nation, husband to a dozen Indian wives, and the best mountain man I know. Aside from all that, I can outride, outshoot, and out lie any man living, with the possible exception of you."

"Now Jim," Augustus said, "I might've stretched the truth just a bit back there in St. Louis, but. . . ."

"Kid, you're a ring-tailed wildcat and the biggest liar I ever had the misfortune of running into, and that's the pure fact of the matter. Come on, we need to get back to the others, it'll be dark. . . ."

"What is it, Jim?" Augustus asked when Beckwourth paused.

"Could be trouble, just stand easy and let me do the talking."

Following Beckwourth's gaze, Augustus spotted a half-dozen Indians approaching on horseback, "Do you know 'em?" Augustus asked.

"Can't say that I do," Beckwourth said, "If it comes to a fight, don't wait for me. If I say run, get the hell out of here."

When the war party rode up, Beckwourth began making signs. Augustus didn't understand, but the Indians did. "They're Bannock," Beckwourth said, "Looking for horses to steal, most likely."

The Indian who seemed to be in charge, indicated they wanted food, and powder and ball for their rifles. Beckwourth told them he was very poor and had no food or powder and ball to spare.

Having never seen a black man before, the Bannock were unsure as to what kind of creature Beckwourth was. Beckwourth was asking about the lead Indian's name. "Says he's called, Muddy Water or Muddy Hole, or some damn thing," Beckwourth said, "I can't really make it out. He's none too friendly, I can tell you that."

"Why don't you tell him you're a member of the Crow nation?" Augustus asked.

"Who do you think they were going to steal the horses from? These laggards are no friend of the Crow, I promise you."

"I was just thinking. . . ."

"Stop thinking," Beckwourth warned, "and smile."

"Smile?" Augustus repeated.

"Yes dammit, smile. You can smile can't you?"

"We ain't scared of some Indian named after a mud hole, are we?" Augustus asked with a big exaggerated smile on his face.

"Yes, we are," Beckwourth said without taking his eyes off the lead Indian, "Keep smiling, and get ready to run."

"Run?"

"Like the devil himself was grabbing at your coat tails."

Beckwourth made sign for another minute until Mud Hole ran out of patience. Seeing it was too late for any more words, Beckwourth let out a banshee-like scream and rode straight into the startled Mud Hole. The collision knocked Mud Hole's horse right off its feet. Plowing through the remaining Indians, Beckwourth spurred his horse down the ridgeline.

Yelling at the top of his lungs, Augustus spurred his horse into the suddenly disorganized war party and ran over the unhorsed Mud Hole. The Indian's horse was just getting to its feet when Augustus went by. In a moment of boldness, Augustus grabbed the horse's halter, wrapped the reins around his wrist, and followed the still whooping and hollering mountain man down the hill.

The men in camp heard Indians approaching and saw Beckwourth and Augustus riding for their lives. Grabbing up their guns, they ran out and met the Indians with a volley of shots. The Indians realizing they were far outnumbered and out gunned, turned away and fled.

"Boy," Beckwourth exclaimed when he saw the stolen Indian pony, "You got more sand and less brains than any other man I know."

"Yeah," Augustus said, in his recently acquired mountain man vernacular, "I'll bet old Mud Hole's madder'n a gut shot grizzly right about now."

"I suspect you're right," Beckwourth said, "Let that be a lesson to you, never let the Indians know you're afraid. As soon as they think they got you buffaloed, you're a goner."

"I'll remember," Augustus said, "You scared the devil out of those Indians."

"Yeah," Beckwourth said with a grin, "Reckon they never seen anything like me before."

True to Beckwourth's prediction, it was early fall by the time they reached the western edge of the high desert. After cresting one of the hills surrounding the Black Desert, a large blue water lake appeared below them. The lake seemed strangely out of place, lying among the arid and steep sagebrush covered hills rolling away in every direction.

A few cottonwoods and juniper bushes grew along the lakeshore. There was a natural formation right on the edge of the lake that very much resembled a pyramid. The eroded dirt and rock cone was a least three-hundred feet high. In addition to the large barren island just offshore, they marveled at the mounds of huge pock-marked and sometimes hollow Tufa Rocks deposited in piles around the area.

John C. Freemont and Kit Carson would arrive at the lake some two years later. Freemont would write exaggerated claims about a six-hundred-foot pyramid and claim to be the first white men to ever see it, but he was hardly the first.

After arriving on the shore, the Fur Company party split into several groups and went off to scout around the lake. Beckwourth and Augustus were riding along the south shoreline when they came upon a small village of Paiute Indians.

This group of Paiutes seemed healthy and happy but they had few possessions. They lived in huts made from reeds that grew around the lake. The weather in the high desert was dry and mild most of the time, eliminating the need for a more substantial lodge.

Beckwourth had been among the Southern Paiutes before and these northern cousins welcomed him into their lodges. After making the formal introductions and bestowing a few gifts on their hosts, Beckwourth and Augustus laid out their bedrolls in an empty hut.

"How is it you know these people?" Augustus asked.

"I've been told about these lake dwellers by other Indians," Beckwourth said. "They're known as Kuyuidokado, or Cui-ui, the fish eater's. Most white men call them the Northern Paiutes."

"Did you see the fur these Indians have?" Augustus asked.

"I did," Beckwourth replied. "It's mostly coyote and rabbit, and besides, these Indians won't allow us to start trapping here. I can't say as I blame 'em, they don't seem to have a hell of a lot. We'll move on toward the mountains in a few days and try to find some virgin territory."

"What are those little white skins?"

"Pelican chicks," Beckwourth replied.

"What's a pelican?"

"Boy, you ask a lot of questions."

"Only way I'll get to be as smart as you," Augustus replied, playing to Beckwourth's ego.

"I suppose, you got a point," Beckwourth said. "Pelicans are big water birds. They come here every year from the Pacific Ocean by the hundreds. Build their nests and raise their young out on that island. The Indians go out there and take some of the chicks for food."

"Why would the pelicans fly all the way over the mountains just to get here?"

"How in blazes would I know that? They're pelicans, it's what they do, that's all I know."

"I wish we could just fly over those mountains," Augustus said, "I'm anxious to see the Pacific and California."

"You flying over those mountains like a bird," Beckwourth said with a chuckle, "You'll never see that, can't be done. Just remember,

Kid, we'll have to walk soft. California belongs to the Mexicans and they ain't real keen on us Americans coming into their land."

"Why don't these Paiutes have any horses?"

"No need, I suppose," Beckwourth replied, "There's no buffalo. This desert country won't support many grazing animals."

"You ever seen the country south of here?" Augustus asked.

"Not much of it," Beckwourth replied, "Why do you ask?"

"My ma told me I was descended from a race of people who lived in the southwest. She claimed they were kings until the Spanish came along and killed most of them."

"I wouldn't know about that, Kid."

"One day, I'm going down there and see for myself."

"I'm sure you will, Kid. I'm sure you will."

Beckwourth and his small party stayed several days with the Paiutes. It was a time for them to rest and restock their provisions. The night before they were to depart, Beckwourth said his goodbyes to the Indians and retired to his lodge.

"What's the matter, Kid?" he asked Augustus, "You look a little pale."

"I ain't feeling too good, Jim. Must've been something I ate."

"Get a good night's sleep. You'll feel better in the morning."

By dawn, Augustus was seriously ill. His fever was high and he was out of his head. The Indians did what they could for him, but it was obvious to Beckwourth the boy might not live through the day, much less travel over the mountains.

It was midmorning when Beckwourth entered the lodge and knelt beside Augustus. "Kid, can you hear me?" Augustus opened his eyes and tried to speak, but he was too weak. "I hate to leave you here," Beckwourth said, "but I got no choice. We got to meet the others and find a way across the Sierras before winter shuts us out."

Augustus tried to raise himself up, but fell back. "I know you want to go, but you're in a bad way," Beckwourth said. "It's a bad break, but every mountain man runs that risk. We'll be back through here next summer. If you ain't dead, maybe I'll see you then. So long, Kid. I was proud to know you."

It was several days later when Augustus finally began to improve. The Indians were giving him a mixture of pinon nut meal, buck berries, desert parsley, and bitterroot. The concoction seemed to be working and his fever finally broke. He was still in and out of consciousness and too weak to even get up, but it appeared he would live.

Just before sundown that evening, he was awakened by excited voices and people running around outside. He was shocked to hear running horses, gunshots, and the shouts of men who were strangers with strange accents. The gunshots were followed with crying and occasional screams from the Paiute women and then all fell silent.

Being weak and lightheaded, Augustus wasn't sure if he was having a nightmare or if the sounds were real. He was struggling to get to his feet when a man with a rifle pulled back the covering of his lodge and looked in. "There's one more still alive in here," he shouted to his unseen companions.

"Shoot him," someone yelled, "He's just another stinking Indian."

Augustus threw up his hands as the man raised his rifle, "No. . . ." he tried to say just as the bullet ripped through his chest.

"Lacourse, how much do you think these furs are worth?" Pierre Barnabe asked. Barnabe was the man who shot Augustus and second in command of the group that had just slaughtered the Indians.

"There's not so much here," Lacourse said, "Just rabbit, coyote, and a few pronghorn." Etienne Lacourse was the leader of this brutal bunch of misfits. They wandered the frontier, taking whatever they wanted, wherever they found it. Indian people were little more than vermin to them.

"Why did we waste time in coming here?" Barnabe asked.

"I did not plan to find these particular Indians, but it is rumored the Paiutes around this lake may have access to riches, perhaps gold and silver," Lacourse said.

"I don't see any gold or silver," Barnabe said, "aside from the furs; all we found are a few of these small pouches."

"Pouches," Lacourse repeated, "what is in the pouches?"

"Pebbles," Barnabe said, "Just these worthless small pebbles." While he spoke, he dropped the stones on the ground and tossed the pouch into the fire. "Why would they keep something like that?"

"Who knows, these people are little more than primitive children," Lacourse said, "We will camp here tonight and rest. Tomorrow we go south. The Indians down there may be richer than these poor dogs."

Lacourse and his raiders were a small but brutal force of a dozen men. They took advantage of the scattered people on the frontier by attacking only small groups and never leaving anyone alive to tell of their deeds. In addition to their male victims, these raiders were responsible for the brutal murders of many innocent women and children from Saskatchewan to the Colorado River.

It was full dark and the moon was up as the raiders sat around the fire bragging about their conquests. The light from the full moon reflecting off the lake made the night bright. In spite of the dead bodies lined up just outside the firelight, they were laughing and doing their best to drink up the last of their whiskey.

None of them knew how far they would have to go or what they would be forced to do to get a new supply, nor did they care. These brutal men were used to living for the present and letting fate take care of the future. Had they known their future was growing short or unimaginable vengeance was headed their way, there would have been little reason for laughter.

Barnabe got up and stepped away from the group to relieve himself. Admiring the moonlight on the lake, he wished they had left some of the women alive a little longer. He smiled to himself as he touched the coin in his pocket. Earlier, he hadn't been completely honest with Lacourse, neglecting to mention the twenty-dollar gold-piece he found in the boy's pocket. In his excitement over the coin, Barnabe missed the golden amulet around Augustus' neck.

As he stood there, Barnabe was confused by the ominous silence. Earlier, the night had been filled with the sounds of waterfowl resting out on the lake and coyotes looking for company in the desert. Now it seemed even the insects were silent.

Just as Barnabe was buttoning up, a rush of wind engulfed him and a fleeting dark shadow resembling smoke rushed by him. "What de hell was that?" Lacourse asked from the campfire.

"I don't. . . ." Barnabe was cut short as another smoky shadow flashed through the camp, scattering sparks from the fire.

"Get to the horses!" Lacourse shouted as yet another larger and almost tangible shadow rushed through the camp. Before the drunken men around the fire could get to their feet, the fleeting wraith descended upon the picketed horses and they bolted away in terror.

The now suddenly sober raiders stood together, guns in hand, staring at the empty and once again silent landscape. Much to their regret, the silence did not last long. A low rumbling sound began to build in volume as three huge shadows appeared on the distant ridgeline and began to descend on their camp.

As the sound increased it began to resemble dozens of running horses. To add to the raider's growing fear, the billowing cloud forming in the wake of the shadows resembled smoke rather than dust. As the ominous shadows drew near, they took the shape of three massive beasts, the likes of which these men had never seen, "Dear God, what devils' spawn is that?" Barnabe asked. The coal black beasts were moving on four legs, but much larger than any horse. The ground underfoot trembled from their thundering gait as they came on like a dark whirlwind.

Lacourse and the raiders paled at the sight of the phantoms sitting astride the charging beasts. Dropping their guns, they began to flee from one another in terror. Lacourse lost his footing and fell just as one of the phantoms caught up with him. The dark figure was tall and dressed all in black when he came to stand over Lacourse. The ominous dark figure was wrapped in a black cape and carried a shining sword.

The figure was manlike, but not completely human. His eyes glowed yellow with narrow vertical pupils as he studied the Frenchman. Unable to move, Lacourse knew he was looking into the face of death. Screaming, he threw his hands over his eyes as the dark warrior issued a thunderous roar, raised the sword over his head and struck Lacourse with the heavy blade.

The other warriors dismounted and took their terrible vengeance on all the scattered raiders. Lacourse's screams were mixed with the others as they reverberated across the lake. Rivulets of blood soaked into the sand along the lakeshore. Dismembered bodies were tossed back and forth as the merciless trio slashed their way through the raiders. The carnage went on until all the raiders were dead and the night was once again silent.

Augustus found himself suddenly awake, feeling a heavy hand on the hole in his chest and staring into the glowing yellow eyes of a dark and formidable stranger. Augustus was outside and lying among a group of dead Indians. Even though the weather was still warm, he seemed to be ice cold as he stared at the dark figure kneeling beside him. Augustus felt he should have been afraid, but for some reason, he wasn't.

The dark warrior pressing him down was dressed all in black and examining the amulet around Augustus' neck. Holding it with his free hand, the dark warrior studied the amulet intently. When the warrior finally spoke, his voice was thunderous, deep and hollow. "You have the blood of a king, the blood of Chimalpopoca, brother of the jaguar."

"I don't. . . ."

"You wear the amulet of Chimalpopoca," the stranger said.

"What do you want?" Augustus asked, attempting to get up.

As he spoke, the eyes of the warrior dimmed and became more human. His voice grew softer, but he continued to press Augustus to the ground. "We are here because of you," he said, "The evil ones are now among the dead, but you, little brother, have a choice."

"What choice?" Augustus asked.

"You can remain here with them," the warrior said, pointing to the dead lying all around, "or you can join us." Two more dark figures came and stood over them in the dark as Augustus pondered the meaning of the warrior's offer.

"All these people are dead," Augustus said.

"That is true."

"I don't want to stay here with them."

"Then you must join us."

"Who are you?"

"I am Perseus," the dark warrior said, "This is Theseus and Orpheus," he added, pointing to the others.

"But what are you?"

"Eternal warriors, known in many cultures," Theseus said.

"In the legends of the Anasazi," Orpheus said, "we are the Riders of the Dire, the sons of Chimalpopoca."

"Who is Anasazi?"

"The Anasazi are the ancient ones," Perseus said, "the people of your grandfathers."

"And what of Chimalpopoca," Augustus asked.

"Chimalpopoca was a king," Theseus said, "a savage warrior, and a powerful shaman.

"As Chimalpopoca was being burned alive, he was forced to witness his family being impaled by the Spanish Iron Bellies," Perseus said, "From the midst of the flames he used his anger and hatred to place an eternal curse upon the Iron Bellies, and all evil men who might follow them into this land. Along with the Dires, we were called from the smoke of that fire, eternal mystic warriors, charged to seek vengeance for Chimalpopoca and his land, but only against the very worst of mankind."

"Know this little brother," Orpheus said, "if you choose our path, your life will not be your own. You will become a man, but never grow old, time and space mean nothing astride the Dires. The weaknesses of mankind, love, pity, mercy, and forgiveness will be unknown to you."

"I will join you," Augustus said to the dark figures around him.

"Then on your feet, brother of the jaguar," Perseus said.

Removing his hand from Augustus' chest, the dark warrior got to his feet and helped the boy up. When Augustus was upright he noticed the ragged hole in his chest was replaced by a scar and warmth had returned to his body

"The powers of evil and darkness seek to devour the earth," Theseus warned.

"Live your life with courage, Son of Chimalpopoca," Orpheus said, "for you are invincible. The evils of mankind will have no power over you."

"One day, when you are ready, and when you are needed most," Perseus said, his hand on the boy's shoulder, "we will return for you."

Chapter Two: The Journey to Manhood

The next morning, Augustus was searching for anything he could find to eat. He knew he couldn't stay there with death all around him. He didn't have the strength to even begin burying all the bodies. In his weakened state of mind, he wasn't sure the dark warriors from the night before were real or a nightmare born from being wounded.

The scar on his chest seemed real enough, but he didn't have time to figure it all out. He planned to put a pack together and start walking west. He had no idea where he was or how far he would have to go to find other white men, but he knew Beckwourth had gone that way and he hoped to catch up with the fur traders.

He was sick to his stomach as he searched through the butchered Frenchman's belongings, looking for whatever he could use. He found his gold piece lying next to what was left of Barnabe.

Augustus found a beautiful .45 caliber Hawken rifle and a couple of flintlock pistols. He would never know the Hawken belonged to Barnabe or that it was the rifle that put the hole in his chest.

During the night a couple of the raider's horses had found their way back to the lake for water. There was an exceptional big black stud among them and he allowed Augustus to walk right up to him. After mounting the big black, Augustus easily caught two more. Now with guns and horses, he was preparing to travel west and find Beckwourth.

As he was searching through one of the lodges, looking for food, he heard a horse outside. Peaking through the openings in the reeds, he saw a young Indian boy leading half-a-dozen horses. "Come out," the Indian said when he noticed Augustus watching him. Augustus was surprised the Indian could speak English.

"I was looking for. . . ."

"What are you doing here?" the Indian asked.

"I was with Jim Beckwourth…fell sick with a fever…they left me here."

"Did you kill all these people?"

"No…no, It was the Frenchmen. Those horses you are leading belonged to them."

"These horses belong to me now," the Indian boy said, "Who killed all of the Frenchmen?"

"I don't know…I was sick…couldn't say."

"Are you planning to stay here?" the Indian asked.

"I'm going to California."

"There is snow in the mountains. You will freeze to death before you can get across."

"I can't stay here," Augustus said, "I must. . . ."

"Come with me," the Indian said, "My father will know what to do with you."

"What's your name?" Augustus asked.

"I am Numaga, son of Chief Winnemucca."

Winnemucca, being a wise and compassionate man, took the kid in to live with his people for the winter. As time went by, Augustus and Numaga became great friends. The two of them hunted together, caught pelicans, and fished for cui-ui and hoopagaih in the lake.

Having no family and nowhere else to go, Augustus stayed with the Paiutes for several years. Finally, at age eighteen, he gave in to his wanderlust, said goodbye to Numaga, and headed off into the mountains. Before he left, Numaga presented him with a large knife as a token of their friendship.

Over the years, Augustus never caught up with Beckwourth. The legendary mountain man seemed to always be on the move to another adventure. Augustus grew into a fine looking man, with the long black hair and dark eyes of his ancestors. He tried his hand at fur trapping for a few years, but the money was gone from that enterprise. Finally, he drifted into California and went to work on a sprawling cattle ranch.

With his name being Alcazar, and with the dark complexion of his father, Augustus fit right in with the Mexican cowboys. He learned a lot from his friends. They taught him all about herding cattle, how to use a riata, and how to be a two-fisted hard-riding vaquero.

The California sun was brutal in the summertime. Finally, one of the old Mexican cowboys took pity on Augustus. One evening after supper, he took Augustus aside. "I am tired of seeing your red ears and sunburned face," he said, "Take my old sombrero. It will keep the sun off your head and keep you cool."

"Thank you, Gregorio," Augustus said, trying on the big hat, "This will be much better." After years of exposure to relentless sunshine, wind, and rain, the slouchy old sombrero had faded to a light tan color with a pronounced darkly stained sweat ring. It wasn't some fancy, serenading guitar player's stiff-brimmed sombrero. Its wide floppy brim, tall crown, and stampede string, indicated it was a working vaquero's hat. Augustus pushed the brim up in front and pulled it down low in the back. "How do I look?" he asked, pulling the string slide up under his chin.

"A lot better than that old bandit ever looked," one of the others said.

"You look like me," Gregorio said, "a real machismo muchacho. You could almost pass for a bandito."

Gregorio Espinosa was a semi-reformed old bandit of some fame around northern California. Gregorio took a liking to Augustus and in the evening, they would talk of many things. The old bandit had lots of stories to tell. Most of the cowboys on the rancho had already heard them and dismissed them as the products of an old man's imagination.

Augustus was different. Intrigued by Gregorio, he was eager to listen to his stories and learn from the old bandit. Over time, they became close friends.

"Gregorio," Augustus asked one evening while they sat on the veranda, "All I have ever used is my old flintlock dueling pistols. I'm not very good with them and they are difficult to load and fire very fast. Could you teach me to shoot your revolvers?"

"Si, I can do that, my young friend," Gregorio said, "Can you get me the bottle of Tequila from the table inside?"

"I can do that," Augustus said, getting to his feet.

"That is muy bueno," Gregorio said after taking a long swig from the bottle. Replacing the cork, the old bandit leaned back against the wall and took in a lungful of the soft matilija scented night air. "There is one thing you must know," Gregorio said, "It is the most important thing."

Pausing for a moment, he took the stub of a cigar from his pocket and stuck it in the corner of his mouth. Taking a match from the other pocket, Gregorio scratched it on the wall behind him.

Tilting his head to avoid burning his nose, the old bandit's cheeks sunk in over his nearly toothless jaw as he pulled on the cigar. Augustus watched and waited as the glow from the match illuminated the deep wrinkles in the old bandito's weathered and worn face.

After the end of the stubby cigar began to glow bright red, Gregorio blew out the match, tossed it aside, and looked back to Augustus. "The deadliest man in the fight is not always the fastest to draw or the first to shoot," he said.

"What do you mean?" Augustus asked.

"The Gringos, they put great value in being...what you call...the fast draw, but that is not the most important thing."

"Can you teach me to be a fast draw?" Augustus asked.

"No, I cannot! Did I say a fast draw was the most important thing?"

"You never said what the most important thing. . . ."

"Perhaps patience is the most important thing."

"Is patience the most. . . ."

"No, it is not! If you would close your mouth and open your ears, perhaps I will tell you what the most important thing is." Taking the not so subtle hint, Augustus stopped talking and sat quietly. "Only practice can teach you to be a fast draw," Gregorio continued. Tendrils of smoke circled the old bandits head as he took another deep draw on the cigar and carefully studied Augustus. "Do you believe I am the most feared bandito in all of California?" he finally asked.

"I do believe that," Augustus said.

"Then I, Gregorio Espinosa, the most feared bandito in all of California, will teach you to be the deadliest pistolaro in any fight."

"How can you do that?"

"Being fast isn't good enough. You must be able to kill your opponent no matter what else is going on around you. You must never let fear enter your mind. Make the others be afraid. You, my friend, must be calm, determined, and most of all; you must let them know you are willing...no...happy, to kill every man in the fight."

"How do I do that?"

"Always carry two pistolas. Most men become very nervous when faced with a man with two pistolas. They begin to think, either he is a very foolish green-horn or he is a very deadly pistolaro. If they think too much, they begin to doubt their abilities."

"I'll remember."

"And then, you look at them like this." The old bandit's face transformed into a snarl as he suddenly sat bolt upright, his face inches from Augustus'. Gregorio's piercing dark eyes barely shown through squinted eyelids as he glared at Augustus. Focused on the old man's face and oblivious of his hands, Augustus suddenly became aware of the cool steel of a pistol barrel poking him under the chin.

"I...I see what you mean," Augustus said as a mixture of tequila breath and cigar smoke washed over him, "I think I can. . . ."

"You think! No, you cannot think!" Gregorio said, grabbing Augustus by the shirt and shaking him. The sombrero fell off Augustus' head and hung between his shoulders as the old man continued, "Thinking will get you killed. Make your enemies think. Be the deadliest man in the fight! The others will know...they will always know."

"I will remember," Augustus promised.

"Good," Gregorio said, letting the hammer down on his pistol and leaning back against the wall, "Tomorrow we begin."

It was early February, 1848, when a Mexican named Philippe Roas showed up at the rancho looking for a job. He was fresh from the war with the Americans and in bad need of money. Philippe had a matched pair of brand new Colt Walker Dragoons that he had taken off an American officer.

Augustus had been saving his money for many months to buy a pistol. After seeing the big cap-and-ball dragoons, he purchased them from the Mexican. The big .44's were heavy, weighing nearly five pounds apiece when fully loaded, packing 60 Grains of powder in each of their six cylinders, but Augustus soon became accustom to carrying them.

Augustus spent hours with the dragoons. Over time, they became like an extension of his body. With the combined philosophy of gun fighting learned from Gregorio and his seemingly natural ability to hit what he shot at, Augustus had all the makings of a deadly Pistolaro.

It was late on a hot Sunday afternoon when Philippe came thundering in on his lathered horse and bailed off in front of the bunkhouse. "Are you trying to kill your caballo?" Gregorio asked the breathless cowboy.

"The gringos…they are taking our cattle."

"Where," Augustus asked.

"From the river, they are going south."

"How many gringos?" Gregorio asked.

"Maybe six…ten, I don't know," Philippe said, "We must hurry."

It was two hours before midnight when Augustus and the cowboys with him found the rustler's camp. "There is only one man guarding the cattle," Gregorio said.

"Stay here," Augustus said, getting down from his horse, "I'll get him." The others watched as Augustus silently made his way through the sagebrush and slipped up behind the dozing rustler. When he was close enough, Augustus leaped upon the rustler and dragged him out of the saddle. When they were on the ground, Augustus pulled Numaga's knife and plunged it into the rustler's throat.

Leaving the dead man lying where he fell, and without waiting for his companions, Augustus made his way up to the rustler's fire. There were six men talking and passing around a bottle of rotgut whiskey when Augustus walked into the firelight.

"Who the devil are you?" one of the surprised rustlers demanded.

"I am here for the cattle," Augustus said.

"You got some sand to be one lonely Mexican," the man said, "But we ain't giving up this herd to the likes of you."

"I'm taking the cattle," Augustus said.

"All right, Mexican," the man said, "I guess I'm gonna have to kill you."

"You won't kill me," Augustus said, pushing his hat back and letting it fall onto his shoulders "but that won't keep me from killing all of you."

"I won't," the rustler repeated, "I guess we'll see about that. Somebody shoot this Mexican son-of-bitch."

Before any of the drunken rustlers could get their guns out, Augustus pulled his dragoons and began firing. Smoke and flame belched from the barrels as Augustus calmly cocked and fired his big pistols. Thunderous reports shattered the quiet night as muzzle flashes reflected in a thick cloud of smoke from the burning powder. The drunken rustlers got off several shots but it was all in vain. By the time Gregorio got to the fire, all the rustlers were dead. Augustus was standing in the firelight, apparently untouched.

"Why didn't you wait for us?" Gregorio asked.

"There was no time."

"You killed them all."

"I did," Augustus said, "you taught me well."

"I think I may have taught you too well," Gregorio said, pushing back his big sombrero.

It was sundown the next day by the time they got the herd back on the ranch. After supper, Gregorio was sitting with Augustus on the porch of the bunkhouse.

"Do you want to talk about last night?" Gregorio asked.

"There is nothing to talk about," Augustus said.

"It was the first time you ever killed a man, no?"

"Yes, it was," Augustus said.

"That weighs heavily on the minds of some men."

"I know it should, but I felt nothing."

"Did you have to kill them all?"

"They were trying to kill me," Augustus said, "I just kept shooting them until they were all dead. Maybe I should feel ashamed, but I felt nothing while I was killing them...I feel nothing now."

"I saw something in your eyes," Gregorio said, "It was as if. . . ."

"It was nothing," Augustus said, turning to the old bandit, "You saw nothing, my friend."

"You have become a dark and dangerous man," Gregorio said, "a dark and dangerous man."

Late the next spring, Gregorio took a tumble off a rank horse and broke his back. The old bandit lingered for only a few hours before he died. With Gregorio gone and feeling the wanderlust once again, Augustus headed east, back across the Sierras.

He was riding through a little valley just east of the mountains on a late summer day when he came across a campsite. There was a heavy mule-drawn wagon and several pack horses, but the camp seemed to be home to just one man. The man spotted Augustus, but instead of picking up a gun, he waved for him to come in.

Augustus approached with caution, unsure of the man's intentions. "Welcome my friend," the big man said. "You are the first person I've seen in weeks."

"Where are you going?" Augustus asked.

"I'm bound for California. The name's Hansen, Gunnar Hansen."

"I'm Augustus, glad to meet you."

"Won't you get down and join me?" Gunnar asked. "Supper is almost ready, and I would enjoy some company."

While they ate, Augustus found out Gunnar was a Norwegian on his way to the gold fields of California. He had spent three weeks at sea getting to New York, and nearly three months crossing the continent.

"Where did you come from?" Gunnar asked, after supper.

"I came out here with Jim Beckwourth," Augustus said, "It's been...I don't know...quite a few years ago."

"The great Jim Beckwourth," Gunnar said, "I have heard many stories about him."

"I'm sure that's true," Augustus said, "I wouldn't put too much stock in most of them."

"What do you do out here?"

"A little trapping," Augustus said, "one thing and then another, whatever it takes to get by."

"Would you like a job, my friend?"

"What kind of job?"

"I need someone to help me through these mountains. I would be willing to pay a good salary."

"That might work out," Augustus said, "I don't have much going on now and cool weather is coming on."

"Splendid," Gunnar said, "Tomorrow we start for the Feather River."

Right after first light the next morning, Augustus was helping Gunnar hitch the wagon. "Why do you need such a heavy wagon to go prospecting?" he asked.

"The wagon carries the tools necessary to harvest the green kind of gold," Gunnar said.

"Green gold, I don't believe I know what you mean."

"I understand the Sierras are covered in thick forests. In Norway, my family and I were loggers. We cut timber and built houses with the logs. The Californian's need lumber for all kind of things, timbers for the underground mines, sluice boxes, cabins, and buildings for the new towns. I, Gunnar will build a mill to provide that lumber and maybe do a little prospecting as well."

"It sounds like a good plan," Augustus said, "If we can get this wagon over the mountains."

"We will get there, my friend, we will get there."

It took them another two weeks before they arrived at a likely looking spot along the Feather River. The ground was reasonably level and surrounded by thick pine forests. They were just north of the newly founded town of Cherokee, California, right in the middle of the gold seekers.

"What's in this crate?" Augustus asked as he was helping Gunnar unload the wagon.

"Books," Gunnar said.

"There must be a lot of them in here," Augustus said, as he struggled with the heavy crate, "Why so many?"

"Can you read?" Gunnar asked.

"A little," my mother taught me.

"Every man must be able to read and write in this modern age. Books represent the collected knowledge of mankind," Gunnar said. "After supper, we will begin your education."

"I already have all the education I need," Augustus said.

"I suppose we will see about that, won't we?"

After setting up the sawmill it wasn't long before they were doing a booming business selling lumber. The money was good and winter was coming on. Augustus decided to stay and work for Gunnar, at least until spring. The miners abandoned the goldfields in the winter. It was quiet in Cherokee, as most of them went to San Francisco to escape the heavy snow.

Being Norwegian, Gunnar was used to working in the cold and deep snow. The winter afforded him time to stockpile lumber in anticipation of the heavy demand come spring time.

When spring arrived, the miners returned. Gunnar and Augustus were working long hours week after week, cutting trees and sawing lumber. Augustus was accumulating a substantial grubstake for whatever his next adventure might be. In spite of Augustus' early resistance, Gunnar persevered with the book learning. Over the next few years, Augustus would become well spoken and knowledgeable about the world around him, thanks to the big Norwegian.

Augustus was in Cherokee one evening having a drink at the saloon when he heard a commotion out in the street. Walking outside, he found a group of four prospectors surrounding a smaller man who seemed to be Chinese. The prospectors had slipped up behind the seemingly meek Chinaman and knocked him to the ground. They were taking turns kicking him as he lay in the dust.

Without a word, Augustus stepped into the street and approached them, but before he could get involved, the nimble Chinaman shook the cobwebs out of his head, sprang to his feet, and delivered a brutal kick to the nearest prospector. The prospector collapsed in a heap on the ground as the small, but deadly, little Chinaman pounced upon the second man. Augustus watched in amazement as the Chinaman defeated all but one of the aggressors.

Before the Chinaman could get to him, the last man came up with a .32 caliber belly gun. Being unarmed, the Chinaman froze. In the blink of an eye, Augustus pulled both dragoons, pointed them at the prospector and cocked the hammers. The prospector stood quiet for a moment staring into the eyes of the newly-arrived and formidable dark stranger. Finally losing his nerve, he dropped his gun and fled.

"Are you all right?" Augustus asked, holstering his guns.

"Yes," the Chinese man replied, "I am in your debt."

"What was all that about?"

"They don't want me here," he explained. "They call me, Celestial, told me to get out of this area. This gold is for Americans, not Chinese."

"Six months ago, half of that bunch probably weren't Americans either," Augustus said. "Do you have a place to stay?"

"I filed a claim, but there is no more shelter. The other's burned my tent and most of my belongings."

"Well, come on home with me," Augustus said, "Me and Gunnar got plenty of room in the mill."

"That is most kind of you," the Chinaman said, "What is your name?"

"Augustus, what's yours."

"I am Chin-Ho."

"Chin-Ho, it's good to meet you," Augustus said, "What kind of fighting was that? I've never seen anything like it."

"It is called Changquan, an ancient form of Chinese self-defense."

"Do you think you could teach some of that to me?"

"My friend, I sense you are a warrior. It would be my privilege to teach you."

True to his good nature, Gunnar was happy to take in Chin-Ho. The Chinaman insisted on working for his keep and he proved to be nearly tireless. Chin-Ho was also a good cook. He taught Augustus to prepare many new and exotic dishes. The three of them lived a good life throughout the spring and on into summer.

Whenever they could get away from the mill, Augustus and Chin-Ho would do a little prospecting. There were many abandoned claims along the Feather River. Miners would work a piece of ground until it failed to pan out or abandon it when word would come of another big strike somewhere else.

One afternoon, they were panning some gravel when Chin-Ho plucked a small pebble from his pan. "That ain't a nugget," Augustus said, "It's a rock."

"You are correct, my friend," Chin-Ho said, "It is not gold, but it is not a rock."

"What is it?" Augustus asked, "I've seen those before. The Paiutes at the lake had some of them, back when I was a kid. I still have a small pouch of them." He watched as Chin-Ho carefully cleaned the mud from the small stone. When it was clean, it resembled a yellowish tinted crystal. Without answering Augustus' question, Chin-Ho placed the small stone on a flat rock, picked up another smaller rock and slammed it down on the little yellow stone.

"Well, it's gone now," Augustus said. Much to his surprise, and upon closer examination, the little yellow stone was unscathed. "Well I'll be," he said, "What kind of rock is that?"

"It is a diamond," Chin-Ho said, "At least two carats, worth much more than gold."

"I've heard of diamonds," Augustus said, "but I thought they came from far away across the sea, and I thought they were clear."

"Diamonds can be found in many places," Chin-Ho said, "Most are clear, but many are yellow. Some are red, orange, blue, and even brown."

"How do you know so much about diamonds?"

"My father deals in precious stones in San Francisco."

"Well, all right then," Augustus said, "Let's find some more."

After years of hard work, the demand for lumber around Cherokee began to dwindle. The prospectors moved on and the money began to dry up. By that time, Gunnar had developed a bad cough that would not go away. He was losing weight and could barely get out of bed some mornings. The big Norwegian closed the mill and arranged to travel to San Francisco in order to find a doctor who might cure him.

Chin-Ho was in possession of a small tin full of diamonds that he found over several years of searching the gravel of the river. He packed up and went with Gunnar, planning to go into business with his father.

Parting with his friends was a difficult decision for Augustus. "You have taught me many things," he said to Chin Ho.

"You have been a good student, my friend," Chin Ho said, "continue on the ancient warrior's path. You have learned much, but there is still much to learn."

"I will," Augustus assured him, "I will never forget you."

"This will help you remember," Chin Ho said, placing a small hand-crafted silver box in Augustus' hands.

"What's this?" Augustus asked.

"A humble gift, for you, my good friend."

Inside was a sentiment and Chin Ho's signature, engraved in Chinese. "Did you make this?"

"Yes, my grandfather taught me."

"I'll keep it always," Augustus said. Turning to Gunnar he took the big Norwegian's hand. "Gunnar, you've been like a father to me. I don't have the words. Thank you just isn't enough."

"I could never have managed without you," Gunnar said. "Promise you'll come and see me when you can."

"I'll try," Augustus promised, "Until then, take care of yourself."

Augustus still had the heart of a mountain man. He certainly could afford it, but he wanted no part of life in the big city. On the first day of May, 1860, he said goodbye to his friends with a promise to come and visit one day and headed east, to the high desert. He didn't know it at the time, but this trip would lead him into a bloody conflict and force him to choose between the white heritage of his mother or the blood of his grandfather's.

Chapter Three: 1860, Return to the Paiutes

"Looky here what I got," the big man said. He had just come through the door, dressed in buckskins and shoving two young Indians girls along ahead of him.

"Where'd you find them?" a drifter at the bar asked. The dusty drifter had just ridden in to Williams Station about an hour before.

William's Station was a Pony Express way-station near the Carson River. It also served as a trading post, saloon, and a less-than-luxurious hotel. The drifter had stopped at the station to get a bite to eat and night's sleep before going on to Virginia City.

"They was swimming naked down at the river," the big man said, "after I saw 'em I just had to have "em, if you know what I mean. I need a room."

"Take whatever's empty," the barkeep said pointing down the hall.

"Anybody else want a taste?" the big man asked, "I don't think I can hang on to both of these wildcats at the same time."

"I believe I do," the drifter replied. "Cassidy's my name," he said to the barkeep, "Just put this on my bill." Cassidy tossed his drink into the back of his throat and followed the big man and the terrified girls down the hallway.

It took Augustus five days to reach the valley just south of Pyramid Lake. It was late afternoon when he rode into the village of Winnemucca. He wanted to renew his friendship with the old chief and Numaga.

When he arrived, the village was in turmoil. Augustus found Numaga right away. "What's going on?" he asked.

"Two days ago, the whites at William's Station took two of our women."

"Took them," Augustus repeated.

"They raped them over and over and then beat them."

"Where are the women now? Are they dead?"

"No, they live, but just barely. When the white men were finished with them, the women managed to escape. Tonight we ride to avenge them. While you have been gone, the white man has taken almost everything from us. From this day forward, if we are to think of ourselves as men, we cannot let this stand."

"Where is Winnemucca?"

"Winnemucca is dead."

"I'm sorry to hear that."

"You must go now," Numaga said.

"I'm going all right," Augustus said, "I'm going with you."

"But we ride against the whites, your people."

"I'm only part white," Augustus said, "My father was descended from the Anasazi. I look a lot more like you, than any white man I ever met."

"Then ride with us, Augustus. But first you must change those white man clothes and get rid of that hat. In the heat of the battle and in the dark, I'm afraid I might shoot you myself."

"Pour me another shot, will you barkeep?" Cassidy asked. Being between jobs, he was still at the station. Cassidy was basically lazy and not prone to taking orders, he seldom lasted more than a month or two at any one place.

Cassidy had a wife and two young sons somewhere back in Missouri, but he hadn't felt the need to get in touch with them for several years. He had been hanging around William's Station for three days and his welcome was wearing pretty thin. The barkeep was beginning to worry that the drifter might try and skip out on his ever growing tab.

Before the barkeep finished pouring Cassidy's drink, a shot rang out from outside. There were only a handful of people in the station that night. Before any of the startled men could react, the glass in the front windows was shattered. More and more shots were being fired at the station as the men inside doused the lights. They frantically tried to board up the shutters as dozens of screaming Indians made a run at the station. In all the confusion the Paiutes managed to set fire to the rear of the building.

The one-sided battle lasted only a short while. By the time the Indians left, the station was fully engulfed with flames. Only Cassidy and two other men were left alive. Since the place was on fire and the barkeep was dead, Cassidy saw no need in paying his bill. In fact, he helped himself to the cash under the counter and took a couple of bottles for the road. As soon as Cassidy was sure the Indians had gone, he grabbed his horse and lit out for Virginia City.

Six days later, Augustus and Numaga were sitting by a fire having a cup of coffee when two young Indians came thundering into the camp. They rode straight to Numaga and jumped off their lathered horses. "The white's…are coming," the smaller one warned, trying to catch his breath. The Indian's name was Charlie Nighthorse.

"Where," Numaga asked, "Did you see them?"

"They were at the station this morning. Now they are coming toward the lake."

"How many?" Augustus asked.

"Maybe a hundred," the other Indian replied. "Smoke Creek Sam," he said extending his hand to Augustus. "Are you going to join us?"

"Damn right I'm gonna join you," Augustus said, "Sam, it's good to know you. I'm Augustus."

"It is good to know you, Augustus."

"Mount up!" Numaga said. "We must meet the white's before they get here."

Two hours later, Augustus and Numaga were hunkered down on a rocky little hill just south of Pyramid Lake. They had crawled to the top in order to try and spot the white man's militia. "There," Augustus said, pointing south.

"I see them," Numaga said. He motioned for Nighthorse to come up and join them. "Take Sam and all the warriors. Retreat back along that canyon to the north."

"Retreat," Night Horse said, "We have four warriors to their one. It is not time for a retreat."

"There is no time for talk," Numaga said, "Do as I say. Divide your warriors on each side of the canyon, but stay out of sight. I will keep

Augustus and ten others here with me. We will begin the fight from here and then run away. When the whites see us run, they will come after us."

"I see the plan now," Nighthorse said.

"Wait until they are all in the canyon, before you strike."

"I will," Nighthorse said. "Today they will all die."

"Be well," Augustus said to Nighthorse.

"You take care, Brother," Nighthorse replied. The young Indian slipped down off the hill and went to the other mounted warriors. Numaga could see a brief council being held between Nighthorse and Smoke Creek Sam. When they were finished, all of them rode quietly away into the canyon.

"How many Indians took part in the raid at William's Station," the man at the head of the column asked. He was dressed in a Union Cavalry Officer's uniform. Cassidy was riding beside him. Cassidy had raised the alarm in Virginia City and a ragtag militia was hurriedly assembled. The militia's leader insisted that Cassidy return with them.

"There weren't no more than thirty of forty of them, Major Ormsby," Cassidy replied. In reality, he had no idea how many Indians had taken part in the raid. He spent most of the time under a table in the dark while the rest of the men fought it out with the Paiutes.

"We should have enough men to handle them," Ormsby said. "We'll push on to the lake before it gets dark."

The militia had only gone another mile when they suddenly found themselves under fire from the little hill. Dismounting, they formed skirmish lines and began firing from the ground. In the heat of battle, Cassidy, determined to put as much distance as possible between him and the fighting, managed to slip away to the rear of the column.

"That's enough," Numaga said after a few minutes, "Let's go."

The Indians with him ran off the side of the little hill exposed to the militia. Many shots were being fired at them, but with little effect. Numaga and his men made it to their horses and bolted up through the canyon.

"Now we got 'em!" Ormsby shouted, "To the horses and after them!"

Thinking this was going to be a glory-filled battle, with a handful of cowardly digger redskins, the militia mounted and spurred their horses after the fleeing Indians.

Ormsby was at the head of the charging column when he began to wonder about the wisdom of his decision. Before he could act on it, his men were overwhelmed by a deadly crossfire of bullets and arrows. Being at the rear, Cassidy could see what was happening to his companions. He turned his horse and managed to escape before any of the Indians could get to him.

Augustus saw him go," I'll get that coward," he shouted to Numaga. Augustus vaulted onto the back of his horse and spurred him after Cassidy.

"Look at this crazy son-of-a. . . ." one of Ormsby's men started to say just as he was struck with a bullet from Augustus. The man on his left watched in terror as the longhaired Indian rode a big black horse straight through the frightened militia. The seemingly bullet-proof warrior was guiding his horse with his knees and firing two big dragoons, killing men on his left and right.

Augustus caught Cassidy just as they broke out into open country at the south end of the canyon. Holstering his dragoons, he rode up beside Cassidy and yanked him off his horse. With the agility of a jaguar and before Cassidy stopped tumbling, Augustus was on him.

"No...no!" Cassidy begged as he crawled across the ground trying to get away. Finally turning to look, he realized Augustus was too big to be a Paiute. "You're no Indian," he said, "Why are. . . ."

He was cut short when Augustus, his pistols empty, landed a mighty blow with a stone club. The vicious blow knocked a bloody chunk out of Cassidy's face. Thinking Cassidy dead, Augustus left him lying where he fell and hurried back to the battle still raging in the canyon.

The running battle lasted all afternoon. Ormsby was wounded but managed to stay in the saddle until he was felled with another bullet a short time later. When it was over, the militia was all but destroyed. Ormsby, along with practically all of his men, was dead.

Only a handful survived to tell the tale. On their way back to Virginia City, the survivors found Cassidy lying bloody, dazed, and nearly dead just south of the canyon.

That night at the Paiute village, Augustus and Numaga sat eating a meager supper. "You must leave here at once," Numaga said.

"Why do you say that?"

"The whites won't stand for what we did to them today," They will come back with an army and you, Augustus, must be far away when they do."

"I suppose you're right, but what about you?"

"We will scatter from here with the dawn. By the time the army comes, we will have crossed the mountains to the east and gone into the Black Desert. They won't follow us out there."

"This may be a good time for me to head south," Augustus said," maybe find some of my ancestors."

"I hope I will see you again," Numaga said.

"I hope so," Augustus said.

Chapter Four: 1867, Carson City

It was a hot day in August, when a well-dressed gentleman by the name of Burton Lee was found sitting outside the Executive Offices in Carson City, Nevada. Burton Lee was a land speculator from Sacramento. He was in Nevada securing land for a right-of-way for the Central Pacific Railroad. "Mr. Lee, the Governor will see you now," the clerk said. He motioned for Lee to follow and led him into the Governor's office.

"Come in, Burton," the man behind the desk said, "Did you have a good trip?"

"Yes Sir, Governor Maxwell, I did." The honorable Milton Maxwell was the recently elected governor of Nevada.

"We need to get to work right away," Maxwell said, "The Central Pacific is ready to start building. We have to get hold of those last few parcels of land. I want a clear right-of-way, two sections wide, all the way across Nevada. It's imperative that no one builds any towns along the way unless we have a say in who runs it."

"I understand, Governor, but. . . ."

"Is there a problem?"

"There are a handful of landowners still holding out. The largest is Jonas Hobbs."

"I'm not surprised," Maxwell said.

"He was one of the first to settle in the valley below Pyramid Lake. He's been there a long time and he refuses to sell us what we need."

"I'm well aware of who Jonas is, but one man can't stop that railroad."

"He offered to grant a right-of-way large enough to lay the tracks, but he won't give us a mile on either side. He claims he would lose too much grazing area and land-lock the northern sections of his ranch."

"That won't do," we must have the entire two miles. You're going to have to convince him to sell."

"I don't think he'll budge. To make matters worse, the smaller ranchers are being influenced by his refusal to sell. One of them is an Indian, claims his land is protected by a treaty with the Paiutes."

"The Paiutes," Maxwell repeated, "No damn Indian is going to hold this up. We need to come down on him hard. Make an example of him, and the other holdouts will see the light."

"I didn't sign up for any violence," Lee said, "This was supposed to be just a business deal. Charlie Nighthorse has a nice family. He's well respected up there."

"You agreed to secure that land and I'm holding you to it," Maxwell said, rising to his feet. "There is too much money at stake to be getting cold feet now. Get back up there and get it done. Get rid of that Indian and his family, and Jonas too, if you have to. I want no more excuses."

After leaving the Governor, Lee returned to his hotel. It was thirty miles back to the little settlement by the Truckee River where he was staying. He had a lot of time to think on the way. Lee decided he was already in too deep to back out and there was a tremendous amount of money at stake.

"Momma, there are men coming up the road," a dark-eyed teenaged girl said. She was peering out the window of their little homestead cabin.

"Christie, get away from that window," her mother warned. "Strangers are never good news. Let your father handle this."

The Nighthorse family lived on a small ranch, just south of Pyramid Lake. Charlie Nighthorse was shoeing a horse in the barn when he heard riders pull up outside. Still holding the shoeing hammer, he walked out to greet them. "What can I do for you men," he asked pushing back his hat and wiping his brow.

"Are you Mr. Nighthorse?" Burton Lee asked from the saddle.

"Charlie Nighthorse, yes sir, that's me."

"Mr. Nighthorse, I'm Burton Lee, from the Great Basin Land Company. I want to talk to you about buying your place here."

"I've already had this discussion with the other men who were out here," Charlie said, "I haven't changed my mind."

"I understand," Lee said, "But it's imperative that you reconsider."

"Why do you want this place so bad?" Charlie asked.

"It's not so much that we want it," Lee said, stepping down, "We need to secure a right-of-way for the Central Pacific Railroad."

"A railroad through this country," Charlie said. "Why here?"

"That's just the way they got it figured," Lee said. "It will run across your place and west to the Hobbs'."

"Have you spoken to Jonas?"

"We have," Lee said, "Just last week."

"Did Jonas sell out?"

"Well, not exactly," Lee said, "But he will, eventually."

"Jonas Hobbs is my neighbor," Charlie said, "He was here first. Jonas has always been a friend to the Paiutes, if he's against this, then I reckon I am too."

"Look, Injun," Wilbur Cassidy warned from his saddle, "This railroad is going to happen and there's little you can do to stop it." Cassidy was working for Burton Lee as a hired gun.

Charlie couldn't help but notice the ragged scar and lifeless left eye of the man that threatened him. "I don't know who you are mister," Charlie said to Cassidy, "But you've worn-out your welcome, now get off my land."

"You think you can run us off with that hammer?" Cassidy asked.

"Seven years ago, my sister was abducted by white men from William's Station," Charlie said, "I rode with Numaga against Ormsby's Militia. When they were driven off and she was finally safe, I vowed no white man would ever hurt my family again."

"Big talk for a man alone," Cassidy said, "But you ain't the only one who was. . . ."

Cassidy was interrupted by a shot fired over his head. Burton Lee was trying to hold his startled horse when he noticed a young woman on the front porch of the Nighthorse house. She had flowing black hair, a blue Gingham dress, and a Spencer rolling-block carbine. Without looking, she deftly inserted a fresh cartridge, closed the breech, and pulled the hammer back, "My daddy said to go! Now go!"

"We're going," Lee said, mounting his horse, "Think about it, we'll talk later."

"No need for any more talk," Charlie said.

"You got a mighty pretty daughter, Injun," Cassidy warned as they were leaving, "Be a shame if anything was to happen to her."

"If you return here," Charlie said, "I will kill all of you." If Charlie had known the badly scarred Cassidy was one of the men who abused his sister, Cassidy would have died right there and then.

"What are you planning to do now?" Cassidy asked Lee as they rode back to the settlement.

"You take a couple of the boys and start making trouble for all the holdouts," Lee said, "If we can scare them bad enough, maybe they'll sell out. I tried to do this right, but now…it's out of my hands. Do whatever you have to. These people have to go and it has to be soon."

Late in the afternoon, three days later and ten miles to the west, two cowpunchers had just ridden up on a disturbing scene. "The old man ain't gonna be happy about this," the first man said. He was down off his horse examining the remains of a freshly killed yearling heifer. Five other carcasses were scattered in the brush nearby. The cause of death was fairly obvious. Each of them had a neat round hole in the middle of their forehead.

"What low down skunk would've done this?" the other mounted cowboy asked.

The man on the ground was Jace Carter, a big outspoken cowpuncher about forty years old and foreman on the Lost Jackass Ranch. The man in the saddle was Jace's saddle partner, Haskell Early. Haskell was a little older than Jace, rough-shod and rugged; he was a man few would want to tangle with.

"Ain't for me to say," Jace said, "But if I had to guess, I'd say it has something to do with the bunch that came by the ranch last week."

"You mean those railroad men? This is 1867; they wouldn't stoop to this kind o' thing nowadays."

"They weren't railroad men, they're land speculators. They were pretty upset when the old man told 'em to go to hell and take their railroad with 'em. They may try to run him out of business if he don't give 'em what they want."

"They're buying up land all over the valley for the transcontinental route," Haskell said, "Claims it'll connect California to the rest of the country, be good for everybody."

"Especially good for the speculators and the Central Pacific," Jace said.

"It only takes a right-of-way about twenty feet wide to lay a rail bed, right?"

"Sounds about right," Jace said.

"Then why are they buying up everything within a mile of the proposed route?"

"I hear the government is giving them a mile on each side where the route crosses public land," Jace said, "The railroad wants the same where they plan to cross private ground."

"If the Old Man sells them a two mile right-of-way, we'll lose the northern third of the ranch,"

"Not only that," Jace said, "we'd lose the best grasslands on the ranch and the water from Wolf Creek, anything north of that right-of-way would be worthless. It'll be land-locked by the reservation and we couldn't get to it."

"I got a bad feeling about this," Haskell said.

"Me too," Jace said, getting back in the saddle, "Right now, let's head to the ranch. The two of us can't do much out there in the dark. We'll get some help and come back up here after daylight in the morning."

Darkness settled in on the Lost Jackass Ranch, just as the cook was putting supper on the table. The fairly substantial man sitting at the head of the table was known to many, but seldom to his face, as The Old Man. Jonas Hobbs was the owner and patriarch of the Lost Jackass Ranch.

Being from Portuguese descent on his mother's side, Jonas Hobbs wasn't a tall man but he was powerfully built. He had a head full of snow-white hair and a thick beard. The testament of his life was etched in the deep wrinkles of his permanently tanned face.

The old man settled in the valley in 1850, right after Jim Beckwourth opened up the pass that bears his name over the Sierras.

The story goes that Jonas was heading to California to prospect for gold until his mule got loose in the middle of the night and headed home to Iowa.

Left without a way to get over the Sierras, and with winter coming on, Jonas decided to stay in the valley and homestead a place for himself. Whether it was true or not, the old man enjoyed telling the story.

Actually, Jonas was a pretty shrewd business man. In 1850, there was a steady stream of emigrants heading across the Sierras to California, many of them from as far away as Missouri. By the time they got to the Truckee River, most of their livestock was worn out from the long and arduous journey.

Jonas began trading in fresh horses, mules, and oxen. After resting and fattening the worn-out animals, he would resell them to the next bunch of emigrants. When he found out a beefsteak was selling for as much as twenty dollars in the mining camps, he began accepting cattle as payment for his fresh animals.

The anticipation of instant riches wasn't there, but raising cattle turned out to be profitable and a much safer bet than digging for gold. Jonas managed to coexist with the few remaining Washoe Indians and the Northern Paiutes. When times got hard for them he would look the other way and allow them to take a steer or two. Over the years, he laid claim to a fair-sized chunk of land.

"Where are Jace and Haskell," Jonas asked.

"They'll be along," the cook said, "you all eat before it gets cold. I didn't spend all day over this damn hot stove just to feed it to the damn dogs."

The head biscuit roller on the Lost Jackass was Tinker Truman. He was even older than Jonas. Tinker was ill-mannered, short-tempered, and always complaining about something or somebody. Nobody knew much about where Tinker came from or how he got to Nevada, and truth be known, they didn't care. They put up with him, because Tinker was one heck of a good cook, and good cooks were worth their weight in gold.

"Pass me one of them damn biscuits," Tom Carter said, mocking the cook. He was sitting across the table from Tinker and poking a little fun at him. Tom was one of the hired hands and Jace Carter's little brother.

"You best start respecting your elders, Boy," Tinker replied, shaking a wooden spoon at the young cowboy, "I'll pass you a damn biscuit...when hell freezes. . . ."

"I'll remind you once more to watch your language at the table when there are ladies present," Jonas said to Tom and Tinker.

"Ladies," Tinker repeated, "What ladies? There ain't been a lady within a hundred. . . ."

While Tinker was yammering on and on, Tom was rolling his eyes and nodding his head toward the only woman at the table, "Ms. Martha, of course," Tom finally blurted out, interrupting Tinker, "you ornery old biscuit roller."

"I'm sorry, Ms. Martha," Tinker said, "Sometimes I forget you're a lady. That is to say...I forget...I mean. . . ."

"It's all right, Tinker," she said, "I accept your apology." Martha Hobbs was Jonas' unmarried daughter and the only woman living on the Lost Jackass. She was in her mid-thirties, tall for a woman and slim of build. Some would call her gangly. She wore no makeup or any frilly feminine under things. Martha wore her hair up under her hat and usually dressed in men's clothes. From a distance she could easily be taken to be just another cowboy. Having been raised without a mother and in the midst of a bunch of rowdy cowpunchers, Martha Hobbs could ride, shoot, fight, and cuss with the best of them.

"Where did your brother go this morning?" Jonas asked Tom.

"He took Haskell and rode to the north end of the range to check on the herd up there."

"Well, they should've been back by. . . ."

"I think I hear 'em," Tinker said before Jonas could finish, "It's about d. . . . It's about time."

"Where you boys been?" Jonas asked when they walked in the kitchen.

"We got a big problem," Jace said without answering the question.

"What kind of problem?" Tom asked.

"Some no-account took the northern herd and stampeded them into the basin on the back side of Dog Skin Mountain," Jace said, "They're scattered to hell-and-gone in that rough country toward the lake."

"Who would've done that?" Jonas asked.

"Beats me," Jace said.

"Did you find any of the cattle?" Jonas asked.

"We found some of 'em," Haskell replied.

"They killed half-a-dozen head up on top, near the Devil's Horns, and just left 'em," Jace said.

"Think it could have been the Paiutes?" Tom asked.

"I don't think so," Haskell said, "Indians might sneak in here now and again, but they'd only kill one and they would've butchered it. This bunch was on shod horses."

"I think whoever did it wanted to make sure we found 'em," Jace said.

"What would they gain from that?" Jonas asked.

"I think it was a warning," Haskell said.

"A warning," Jonas repeated, "From who? About what?"

"The bunch that tried to buy the north range last week," Jace said. "Me and Haskell think they may start causing trouble until they run us off or convince you to sell."

"The word around the country is they're a pretty determined bunch of land grabbers," Tom said, "I hear they threatened Charlie Nighthorse's family the other day."

"Well, I'll tell you all one damn thing," Jonas declared, suddenly on his feet, "If them money grubbing sons-o-bitches are looking for a war, they've damn sure come to the right place."

"You're mighty right about that," Jace said, "As soon as we get the cattle back, we'll go pay 'em a visit and. . . ."

"Hold on," a young man at the end of the table said, "Everybody just hold on." The cool-headed youngster's name was Clay Hobbs, Jonas' twenty-seven-year-old son. "We have no proof it was anybody connected with the railroad. If we go off half-cocked and start a range war, it won't do anybody any good. I say we put men out around the ranch at night and try to catch 'em in the act, then we'll know who to fight."

"I guess that makes sense," Jonas said, returning to his seat.

"After supper, Jace and I will set up a schedule," Martha said, "As soon as you get the north herd back, we'll start watching them day and night. After you eat, you boys get some rest. Starting tomorrow, you may not be getting much sleep. Now pass me one o' them damn biscuits."

That same evening, Burton Lee and a group of his men were sitting at a table in the Red Dog Saloon in a small settlement alongside the Truckee River. The newly established town was being built next to Charles Fuller's toll bridge. The little town of Reno, Nevada wasn't much to talk about as yet, but it was growing. Like most of the buildings in town, the Red Dog was little more than a wooden floor with canvas for the walls and the roof, but it was the only place for miles around to get a drink.

The men were throwing down some locally produced rot-gut whiskey and playing a round of cards. "How did it go out at Hobbs' last night?" Lee asked.

"We hit the herd up on his north border and drove them down through the basin," Cassidy said. "It'll take 'em a couple days to get those cows out of that brush country."

"Do you think that was enough to scare Hobbs into selling?"

"No, the only way that old man will ever leave is feet first." Cassidy had worked for the Hobbs' family at one time; until he decided punching cows was just too much work. "What we've done so far ain't gonna get it done with these people around here," Cassidy said, "If you want to meet the railroad's deadline, we have to get serious."

"We'll meet the deadline," Lee said, "This railroad is important to the whole country. We have to get the right-of-way secured before the construction crews arrive."

"Look here, Mr. High and Mighty," Cassidy said, "We all know you'll be a rich man when this job is done. Don't make out this is all just for the betterment of the country."

"That may be true," Lee said, "But if you don't start getting some results, nobody is going to get paid, including you."

Early the next afternoon, Jace, Haskell, Clay, and Tom were in the big basin rounding up their stray cattle. It had taken most of the morning to make the ride and locate the lost herd. Just as Haskell had predicted, the cattle were well off the ranch and scattered all through the brush-covered basin.

"I think this is about all of them," Clay said to Tom. They were on the west side of the basin with a hundred head or so.

"I believe you're right," Tom agreed, "Lets head 'em east and meet Jace on the other side."

It was just after sunset when the men met on the eastern edge of the basin. They put the herd in a little boxed canyon and made camp at the mouth. They planned to start for the ranch at first light.

After a bite of supper they were relaxing around the fire. It was full dark and the night was warm. Jace rolled himself a quirley and struck a match to light it. "One of you boys take the first watch," he said with smoke curling around his head, "I'll spell you in a couple of hours."

"I'll go," Clay said, "You old timers need your rest."

"Old timers," Haskell repeated, "I hope you ain't talking about me."

"And you damn well better not be talking about me," Jace added with a grin. Clay was the boss' son, but he always made a point to do more than his share and the cowboys all respected him for that.

Clay had been gone about an hour when Jace heard one of the horses grumble out in the dark. "Is he back already?" Haskell asked.

"I don't think its Clay," Tom said, "It's too early for. . . ."

"What are you men doing out here?" a voice demanded from the darkness. Tom's hand went to his rifle. "You best just let that be," another voice warned.

"Who wants to know?" Jace asked, motioning for Tom to stay still. Jace had no way to know how many men were out there in the dark and he didn't want to start anything until he knew their intentions.

"I'll be asking the questions," the voice said as four men walked into the light. They were all armed and holding a pistol on the Lost Jackass crew. The one doing the talking had a big scar through his gnarled eye, "Now what exactly are you doing on railroad property?"

"Railroad property," Jace repeated, "This is open range."

"Not anymore," Cassidy said. "You boys are welcome to spend the night, but you need to get out of here at first light. And don't even think about taking our cattle with you when you go."

"Your cattle," Tom said, "Those beeves all belong to Old Man Hobbs."

"They been grazing on our land," Cassidy said, "That makes 'em ours."

"I don't know who the hell you think you are," Haskell said getting to his feet, "But we ain't leaving those cows behind."

"Then you'll just have to die here with 'em," Cassidy said, raising his pistol. Before Cassidy could pull the trigger, a shot rang out from the darkness. Cassidy was hit in the shoulder as Haskell dove for cover. Tom and Jace pulled their guns and opened up on the remaining three gunmen. The gunfight lasted only a moment. By the time it was over, a dozen shots had been fired and three of the railroad men were dead. In spite of being wounded, Cassidy had managed to slip away in the dark. A moment later, they heard fading hoof beats as he made his escape.

"Is everybody all right," Clay asked when he walked into the light of the fire.

"You got here just in time," Jace said, as he and Haskell stood up.

"What's the matter with Tom," Clay asked.

Turning to his brother, Jace saw Tom was still down. When they got to him, they discovered Tom had been shot in the chest and he was in bad shape. "We got to get him to the ranch," Jace said, "Saddle my horse."

When Jace was in the saddle, they boosted Tom up behind him. "You two gather that herd and head for the ranch at first light, I'll see you there." With that, Jace turned his horse away and spurred him into the night.

"What happened out there last night?" Burton Lee asked while the doctor worked on Cassidy's wound. The gunman had ridden all night to reach the settlement.

"That bunch from the Hobbs' ranch jumped us in the dark. They come out of nowhere and started shooting."

"Were you on their land?"

"No," Cassidy said, "We were well within the railroad property."

"That doesn't seem right to me."

"I've been telling you, we need to come down hard on them. They started a war last night by killing our men. We're gonna need more guns if you want to win."

"What do you have in mind?" Lee asked.

"I'll ride up to Virginia City and hire some men."

It was just after sundown when Clay and Haskell rode into the ranch. They left the herd just north of the house where they figured they would be safe. After turning their horses loose in the cavvy corral, they made their way to the house.

Things were strangely quiet when they walked through the door. Jonas and Tinker were sitting at the table with Jace and Martha. Jace had his face in his hands and Martha was patting his shoulder.

"What's all this," Haskell asked.

"How's Tom?" Clay asked before anybody could answer.

"He's gone, boys," Jace said without looking up.

"Gone!" Clay repeated pulling off his hat.

"He never done nobody any harm," Jace said, "and they just shot him down like a dog."

"Somebody's gonna damn well pay for this," Haskell said.

"Get some fresh horses and let's go find him," Clay said.

"Go find who?" Jonas asked.

"The man that got away," Clay said.

"We don't know who he is."

"I know who he is," Clay said.

"Who," Jace and Jonas said together?

"That ugly son-of-a-bitch, Wilbur Cassidy."

"Who's Wilbur Cassidy?" Jace asked.

"A no good drifter that worked here for awhile," Jonas said, "Before you and Haskell ever got here."

"None of you are going anywhere tonight," Martha said. "We need to give Tom a decent burial and then figure this out before we make a move on Cassidy and whoever sent him."

"After we take care of Tom in the morning," Jonas said, "Martha and I will ride to Carson City to see the marshal about swearing out a warrant for Cassidy. Jace, you and Haskell, gather the southern herd and move them to the range nearer the house. They'll be safer there until we can get this worked out. Take Clay with you and be careful."

Chapter Five: Dinner with the Governor

"Are you the marshal?" Jonas asked as he walked through the door of marshal's office in Carson City.

"Yes sir," the man behind the desk said, getting to his feet, "Deputy U.S. Marshal Ted Webster, what can I do for you?"

"Marshal Webster, I'm Jonas Hobbs from the Palomino Valley, this is my daughter, Martha."

"It's good to meet you Mr. Hobbs, Ma'am. Please have a seat."

After Jonas and Martha were seated, Marshal Webster sat down behind his desk. "We're here to swear out a warrant for a man named Wilbur Cassidy," Jonas said.

"What did this Cassidy do?" Webster asked.

"Destroyed some of my cattle and murdered one of my cowhands."

"Murdered," Webster repeated, "How did it happen?"

"Some of my men, including my son, were on open rangeland just south of Pyramid Lake when Cassidy jumped them in the dark."

"Jumped them, do you know why?"

"I can't prove it, but I believe Cassidy and his men killed several head of cattle on my land and then ran the rest out into the brush country around the lake. The next day, when my men went out there to round them up, Cassidy confronted them. He told my men they were on railroad land and claimed my herd."

"Is it railroad land?"

"As far as I know it isn't," Jonas said, "And that really isn't the point."

"No, of course not," Webster said, "I'm just trying to get as much information as I can. Are there any witnesses who will swear Cassidy was the man who did the killing?"

"Three of our men, including my brother were there," Martha said. "They'll all testify that Cassidy was the one who killed Tom."

"Tom?"

"Tom Carter," Martha said, "The man that was killed."

"What do you plan to do about it?" Jonas asked.

"I'll ride up there in a day or two and see what I can find out. Do you know if Cassidy's still around anywhere?"

"If I knew where he was," Jonas said, "I wouldn't be here."

"What does he look like?" Webster asked.

"You can't miss him," Jonas said, "He's got a big scar on the left side of his face and a gnarled eye."

"We believe he's working for the land speculators who are trying to buy our ranch," Martha said, "I think the man in charge is named Lee. Yes, that's it, Burton Lee."

"Burton Lee," Webster repeated as he was writing. When he was finished he laid the report aside and got to his feet. "Alright, Mr. Hobbs, I think that just about does it. I'll be in touch."

"Good day, Marshal," Jonas said, getting to his feet, "Let us know when you find Cassidy."

"I'll do that, Mr. Hobbs. Are you going to be in town long?"

"Just tonight," Jonas said, "We'll be headed back in the morning."

"Where are you staying?"

"The Nugget Hotel," Martha replied, "just down the street."

"I don't hold out much hope in him finding anybody," Jonas said when they were outside.

"He seemed awfully complacent about a murder," Martha said.

As soon as Jonas and Martha were out of sight, Marshal Webster got on his horse and rode to the Executive Office Building. "Is the Governor in?" he asked when he was inside.

"I'll see is he's available," the clerk at the desk said.

"He better be available," Webster said, "tell him this is urgent."

The clerk returned in just a moment, "You can go right in, Marshal."

"What's so important for you to come barging in here?" Maxwell asked.

"You'll never guess who's in town."

"I don't have time for guessing games, who is it?"

"Jonas Hobbs!"

"Jonas, what's he doing here?"

"He swore out a warrant for one of Lee's henchmen."

"A warrant," Maxwell repeated, "What did he do?"

"Stole some of Jonas' cattle and murdered one of his cowhands."

"This may be the break we needed," Maxwell said.

"How could this possibly. . . ."

"You'll go up there and make a big show of finding the man who did this and bring him to justice. Let Jonas know that law and order will prevail in this state as long as I'm governor."

"I already know it was Wilbur Cassidy, so does Jonas."

"That does create a problem." Maxwell sat down behind his desk and scribbled a note. "Take this to Jonas."

"What is it?"

"It's an invitation to dinner at the mansion, tonight."

Jonas was stretched out on his bed, taking a nap, when he was awakened by a knock at the door. Opening it, he was surprised to find Marshal Webster. "What can I do for you?" Jonas asked.

"This is for you," Webster said, handing Jonas the note.

"What's this?"

"Governor Maxwell would like to invite you and Ms. Martha to have dinner this evening at the mansion."

"What's Milton got on his mind?"

"I'm afraid you'll have to ask him yourself. Can I tell him you'll be there?"

"Yeah," Jonas said, "We'll be there."

Jonas and Martha left the hotel just before seven and walked the four blocks to the Governor's Mansion. "You look good in a dress," Jonas said as they walked along.

"Thank you," Martha said, "But don't get used to it. These things don't work very well on horseback."

"You need to forget about horses and find some nice young man. I need some grandchildren."

"I'm not taking on the upkeep of some worthless cowpuncher just so you can have a houseful of screaming grandkids. If you want grandchildren, you best be talking to Clay."

Arriving at the mansion, a butler dressed in tails met them at the door, "Mr. Hobbs, Ms. Hobbs, welcome to the mansion. The Governor is in the drawing room. Please follow me, this way."

"Jonas," Maxwell said when they walked in the room, "It's so good of you to come."

"Governor," Jonas said, extending his hand, "It's been a long time."

"Please, it's Milton. We've been friends for too long to worry about titles. Who is this you have with you?"

"This is my daughter, Martha."

"Martha, it is indeed a pleasure."

"Thank you Governor, It's very nice to be here."

Later, as they sat over dinner, Maxwell finally got around to business. "Jonas, they tell me you've had some trouble up in the valley."

"There's been a lot of trouble," Jonas said, "Ever since this talk about a railroad started."

"The railroad will be good for this state," Maxwell said. "We all need to work at making it a reality."

"I'm not opposed to a railroad," Jonas said, "but I don't intend to give up half my ranch to see it built."

"They offered to buy your land, isn't that right?"

"Sure, they made me an offer, but I'm not selling. They want a strip, two sections wide, all the way across my ranch."

"From what I hear," Maxwell said, "That's customary. It gives them enough land to develop and make a return on their investment."

"It makes all of them rich men," Jonas said.

"That's probably true enough, but it is a huge investment to build a railroad."

"If I sell them what they want, it'll cut a two-mile-wide swath all the way across my best grassland. That's ten square miles of my ranch. I'm not going to do it."

"Jonas, one man can't stop this railroad."

"I guess that remains to be seen," Jonas said.

"I beg your pardon, Governor," Martha said, "but you seem to have a great deal of interest in seeing this thing done. Do you stand to gain anything from the railroad?"

"I can tell you're Jonas' daughter," Maxwell said. "As governor of this state, of course I want to see it go through."

"That really didn't answer my question," Martha said.

"I'll do all I can to help the people up there in the valley," Maxwell said, "But you can't stop progress."

"Thanks for supper," Jonas said, suddenly wiping his mouth with a linen napkin and getting to his feet, "Good evening."

"Leaving so soon?" Maxwell asked.

"I think we're done here," Jonas said.

"Then, good evening to you, Jonas," Maxwell said, "Ms. Hobbs."

"Governor," Martha replied.

"What do you make of that?" Martha asked as they walked back to the hotel.

"I've known Maxwell for a long time," Jonas said, "I promise you; he's in this thing up to his eyeballs." They left Carson City the next morning and headed back to the Lost Jackass.

Things were quiet for the next week. The Lost Jackass riders watched their herds day and night, but nothing more was heard from the land speculators. There was no indication that the law was even looking for Wilbur Cassidy.

Little did the Hobbs' know, but Wilbur Cassidy was only twenty miles away in the Red Dog Saloon. He had just ridden in from Virginia City with Lee's new army of gunmen. "This is Burton Lee," Cassidy said making the introductions. "He's the man I told you all about."

"Glad to meet you," Lee said to the group, "You boys made good time from Virginia City. Bartender, give these men whatever they want and put it on my tab."

"Much obliged," Cassidy said moving past Lee and heading to the bar. The rest of his men followed him.

As he and Cassidy were standing at the bar having a drink, Lee was curious as to what Cassidy's next move would be. "Now that we have these men, what are you gonna do?"

"We're gonna start with that Indian," Cassidy said, "Then we'll go after Jonas Hobbs."

Charlie Nighthorse and his wife were preparing to retire when they heard the sound of horses and men's voices outside. Charlie went to the fireplace and took the Spencer down from the mantle. "Get back in the bedroom and stay down," he ordered his wife and daughter.

Shocked to see the glow of flames in the front window, Charlie jerked open the door and stepped out on the porch. There were a dozen raiders in the front yard and they had set fire to the house. Before Charlie could react, half-a-dozen shots rang out and he went down.

Charlie lay mortally wounded in the yard as the raiders stepped over him and went in the house. His last moments on earth were filled with the horror of his wife and daughter's screams.

The raiders left no one to tell the tale of their atrocities. Mrs. Nighthorse and Christie was stripped nude and paraded around in front of their burning house. After the raiders tired of their game, several of them had their way with the women. Before they rode off, the raiders murdered the women and left their bodies lying beside Charlie's. It was three days before a cowboy happened to be riding by and noticed the wheeling buzzards.

Word rapidly spread throughout the area about the Nighthorse family and what had happened to them. Some tried to blame the murders on other Indians, but the obvious presence of shod horses soon laid that to rest.

Jace and Clay were on their way back from the south range when they met a heavily-loaded south bound wagon on the road. The man driving was a neighbor of theirs.

"Albert, what's all this?" Clay asked.

"We're leaving," Albert said, "Some men came by and offered to buy us out."

"And you sold?" Clay asked.

"They didn't give us much choice. We've been doing little more than starving ever since we been out there. Ma was ready to go back home. There was a bad looking bunch with Mr. Lee and after hearing what happened to Charlie Nighthorse and his family, well, I figured it best to let 'em have the place."

"Sorry to hear that," Jace said, "what happened to Charlie?"

"You haven't heard?" Albert said. "Last week, Charlie was shot dead, Mrs. Nighthorse and Christie murdered."

"Murdered!" Clay repeated.

"Yes sir," Albert said, "And the place burned to the ground."

"Something has to be done about this," Jace said.

"Maybe so," Albert said, "But not by me, I'm headed out of here."

"We're mighty sorry," Clay said.

"Clay," Albert said, "I hate to say this, but Jonas may be next."

"What do you mean, next?"

"That land speculator had some rough-looking men with him. I overheard one of them mention your place while they were leaving."

"Thank you for that," Clay said.

"Good luck to you," Jace said as Albert stirred up the team and started down the road.

"What do you think about that?" Clay asked as they watched the wagon depart.

"It's gonna get real bad around here, I'm afraid," Jace said. "Charlie Nighthorse was holding out because of Jonas. Unless I miss my guess, and after what Albert just said, we very well could be next."

"Let's get to the house and warn the rest," Clay said. Spurring their horses into a run, the two of them left the road and started cross-country toward the ranch house.

"I can't believe that kind of violence has come to this country," Martha said after Clay explained what happened. "Poor Mrs. Nighthorse and Christie...I just can't. . . ."

"It seems there's a bad bunch roaming the night around here," Jace said.

"Let's do a little roaming of our own," Haskell said, "We shoot a few of them night riders and maybe they'll change their mind about coming out here."

"No, there aren't enough of you," Martha said, "You need to stay close. None of you needs to be out alone."

"Martha's right," Jace said, "According to Albert; the tracks around the Nighthorse's were made by a small army. As much as I'd like to find and kill all of them, we need to go slow. They're probably hoping we'll come looking for them and give 'em a reason to kill all of us."

"We're safer here than anywhere," Tinker said, "We got enough grub to hold up in here for quite a while if need be."

"That's all well and good," Jonas said, "but first thing in the morning, we're going to that new town and see Mr. Lee."

"It's about damn time," Jace said.

At first light, Jonas left the ranch with Clay, Jace, and Haskell. The four of them made the ride to Fuller's bridge and found the office for the Great Basin Land Company. After his lumber order finally arrived from Portola, Lee contracted to have the small false-fronted building put up on one of the town lots. It was near the Red Dog Saloon.

"What can I do for you gentlemen?" Lee asked when they came through the door.

"I'm Jonas Hobbs. You owe me five hundred dollars."

"Mr. Hobbs," Lee said, "I'm glad to finally meet you. Five hundred dollars, I don't understand."

"Your men killed some of my cattle the other night and ran the rest off into the brush country. It took three days and the life of a good boy to get 'em back."

"I'm afraid I don't know anything about that," Lee said. "Have you reported it to the marshal in Carson, City?"

"You're a liar," Jonas said without answering Lee's question. "Your man Cassidy ambushed my men out there on open range."

"No, that isn't right," Lee said, "Cassidy was on railroad land. Your men attacked him."

"I thought you didn't know anything about it." Clay said.

"Well, I might have heard something, I guess I forgot."

"You best remember this," Jonas said, his finger in Lee's face, "If you or Cassidy show up on my land again, you won't live long enough to leave."

"I don't like being threatened," Lee said. "This railroad project is important to the governor of this state. You can't stop him. Governor Maxwell has ways of dealing with people like you."

"I've known Maxwell since he was a clerk in the land office," Jonas said, "I don't know how he got to be governor, but he has no say over. . . ."

"What's going on in here?" Cassidy demanded when he walked through the door. He was startled to find Jonas standing in Lee's office.

Without saying a word, and before Cassidy could get his gun out, Haskell lashed out with a hard right fist and caught Cassidy on the chin. The stunned gunman was knocked back outside, rolled into the dirt of the street and lay still.

"Guess he'll knock next time," Clay said with a grin.

"Is there any law in this town?" Jonas asked.

"Law," Lee repeated, "What for?"

"That man, Cassidy, is wanted for murder," Jonas said, "The marshal from Carson City is looking for him."

"There's no lawman here," Lee said.

"Then, we'll hang him ourselves," Jonas said.

"You ain't hanging anybody, Old Man," a voice said from the street.

When Jonas and his men walked outside, they were confronted by nine men, each holding a rifle. One of them was helping Cassidy to his feet. "You...get out of town," Cassidy said, holding his jaw, "Before we shoot you down in the street."

"There'll be no killing here today," Lee said emerging from his office. "Please, Mr. Hobbs, just go. Let the law deal with Cassidy, if he's really wanted."

Jonas knew some, if not all of them, would die if he pushed it any further. He motioned for his men to follow him and stepped up on his horse.

"This ain't over," Cassidy said when they were in the saddle. "You can bet on that," Haskell replied.

Chapter Six: The Reno Kid

It was just before sundown a week later when Jonas heard horses coming at a run. "May be trouble," he said to Tinker while making his way to the door. He got there just in time to see Clay and Haskell come to a sliding halt and bail off their horses.

"We got company," Clay said as he ran through the door."

"What kind of company?" Jonas asked.

"The worst kind," Haskell said as he started closing the shutters on the front windows.

"At least a dozen riders, coming this way," Clay said, "Armed to the teeth and carrying torches."

Jace came running through the door from the corral. "There's an army coming down the road."

"Get ready," Jonas said, blowing out the lamp, "This is it. Don't be shy, when it starts, kill as many as you can, as fast as you can kill 'em. Martha, you get down in the root-cellar."

"Not likely," she said, working the lever on her Henry .44 rim fire.

They watched as a column of riders rode into the ranch yard and spread out in front of the house. The one in front was easy to recognize. "Hello in the house!" Cassidy yelled.

"What do you men want here?" Jonas yelled through the shutter.

"We don't want anything," Cassidy said, "You may remember me."

"Can't say that I do," Jonas said, "Neither you, nor any of that scum with you."

"Scum," Cassidy repeated, "That weren't very neighborly."

"That's Cassidy," Clay said.

"I know who it is," Jonas said without turning around. "You planning to use those torches or are you boys just scared of the dark?" he shouted to the men outside.

"We're not scared of anything," Cassidy said, "We're here to kill you and take this ranch."

"I don't believe I'm gonna let you do that."

Emboldened by the success of their raid on the Nighthorse Ranch, the men outside began to laugh among themselves. "You got some sand, Old Man," Cassidy said, "Seems a shame to kill all of you. Is Ms. Martha in there?"

"What's that to you?"

"Send her on out and we'll make sure she's well cared for."

"Yeah," another raider yelled, "Well cared for." The raiders once again began to laugh.

"Like you cowards cared for the Nighthorse women?" Jonas shouted.

"I wouldn't know about that," Cassidy said, "But I heard the young one enjoyed it."

"Yeah," one of Cassidy's men said, "right up until we slit her. . . ."

Before the mouthy braggart could finish, a shot rang out from behind the cavvy corral driving him backwards out of the saddle.

"What the devil was that?" Jace asked.

"I don't rightly. . . ." Jonas was cut short as multiple shots began coming from the unseen gunman by the corral. "Pour it in 'em!" Jonas yelled as the battle began.

Jonas could see the raider's growing panic in the glow of their torches. Suddenly confronted by the deadly gunfire from the corral and with his men falling all around him, Cassidy managed to turn his horse and flee. Most of the remaining raiders were in a battle for their lives amid panicked horses and didn't see him go.

Dozens of shots were being fired from outside, but few of them seemed to be aimed at the house. After only a few minutes, everything outside grew deathly quiet.

"Hold your fire," Jonas ordered, "Hold your fire."

"What just happened out there?" Tinker asked.

"I don't...rightly know," Haskell said, peering through the shutter.

"Hello in the house!" a stranger's voice yelled, "It's over. It's all right, I'm a friend!"

"Who do you suppose that is?" Tinker asked.

"Could be a trick," Haskell said.

"It's no trick," Clay said. He was at a side window and the only one in the house who could see the cavvy corral. "There are dead men all over out there. The big man by the corral is the only one left standing."

"He wasn't with those others," Jace said after joining Clay at the side window.

They nervously watched and waited to see what the stranger with the large sombrero and long dark duster was going to do. "Look at that hat," Clay said, "he must be a bandit, Mexican maybe."

"He's too tall to be a Mexican," Haskell said.

"Let's go find out who he is," Jonas said, "But watch him." Opening the door, he stepped outside. "What are you doing out here?" Jonas asked the stranger while the others held their guns on him.

"I was just passing by...thought you folks could use some help."

"You couldn't have picked a better time," Jonas said, "How many are with you?"

"It's just me," the stranger said.

"There was a lot of shooting out there for just one man," Jace said.

"Yeah, well...this bunch did most of the shooting."

"How did you manage to kill all of them and not get yourself shot?" Haskell asked.

"Just lucky, I guess. I think you all got a couple of them. The rest of them took off before I could get to 'em. Sorry for letting 'em get away. Do you suppose I could come on over there and maybe we could stop yelling at each other?"

"The man's right," Jonas said, "Put down your guns. Come on in!" he shouted to the stranger.

When the stranger started toward the house, they noticed he was being followed by a big black horse. After tying his horse to the rail, the stranger stepped up on the porch. "Thanks for your help," Jonas said extending his hand.

"You're welcome," the stranger said, shaking Jonas' hand and pulling off his hat, "It looked a little one sided from where I was." The tall stranger looked to be in his mid-forties. He was clean shaven with chiseled features, a lean build, and a strong voice. He wore his raven black hair long like an Indian.

"And just where, exactly, was that?" Haskell asked.

"Up on the hill back there. I managed to work my way down to the corral while they were yelling at you."

"What's your name, stranger?" Martha asked pushing past her father.

"My friends call me Augustus, ma'am," he said, taking her hand, "Pleased to make your acquaintance."

"Likewise," Martha said, "We don't get much company. . . ."

"What do others call you?" Haskell asked.

"Just Augustus," the stranger replied.

"You got a last name, Augustus? It just seems a little too. . . ."

"Augustus will do," Jonas said, before Haskell could finish. "Come on in, we were just fixing to sit down to supper, you can join us."

"What about those men outside?" Martha asked.

"Leave 'em," Jonas said, "We'll get rid of them in the morning."

"That was the damnedest thing I ever saw," Tinker said as he was putting supper on the table. "Augustus, you must be about the best gun hand I ever heard tell of."

"Or the luckiest," Haskell added.

"Probably the luckiest," Augustus said.

"Deadly and modest," Martha said, "A rare combination these days."

"What's that supposed to mean?" Clay asked.

"I mean most gunmen go around bragging about their reputation," Martha said, "Augustus here seems different somehow."

"Augustus seems just a little too good to be true," Haskell said. "It's mighty suspicious he showed up the same time as the raiders."

"What about that?" Clay asked.

"It's like I said, I was passing through and saw the raiders."

"Passing through to where?" Clay asked.

"To wherever time and circumstances take me."

"Are you looking for work?" Martha asked, "We're a little short-handed."

"I would like to stay around for awhile," Augustus said, "Till all this trouble is settled."

"What trouble might that be?" Haskell asked.

"Those men that were out front with torches a little while ago for starters, I doubt whoever sent them is finished with you."

"What would you know about that?" Jonas asked.

"I hear things," Augustus said, "there are some really bad men running around this country right now. There are riches to be had and riches bring out the worst in some men. It will take good men willing to do violent things to stop them."

"He's right about that," Jace said to the others.

"You're welcome to stay here," Jonas said, "We could use another hand."

"Where are you from?" Clay asked.

"Missouri, originally," Augustus said, "I came out here with Jim Beckwourth."

"Beckwourth," Jonas said, "That blow hard. You don't seem old enough to have ridden with Jim."

"I was thirteen when we got here. My mother died, leaving me an orphan, and Jim just took me under his wing for a spell."

"That's a mighty interesting story," Tinker said scratching his chin.

"Speaking of being from somewhere," Augustus said, "What's the name of that one-horse town they're trying to start down by Fuller's bridge? It wasn't there the last time I rode through here."

"I think they're gonna call it Reno," Jace said, "After some Civil War hero."

"What are they thinking," Tinker asked.

"What's who thinking?" Clay asked.

"The people in town," Tinker said, "it ought to be named after somebody who's at least been out here."

"What do you think they should call it?" Clay asked, "Tinker Town."

"Tinker Town," Tinker repeated, rubbing his whiskered chin, "Now that ain't too damn bad."

After supper, the cowboys excused themselves from the table and headed for the bunkhouse. "I want to know one more thing," Clay said to Augustus before he got to the door.

"What's that?" Augustus asked, turning back.

"Where in hell did you get that hat?"

"This thing," Augustus said, hat in hand, "It was a gift...from the most feared bandit in all of California."

"I figured it had to be a gift," Haskell said, "Nobody would spend good money on that hat."

"If the old bandit wore that hat," Clay said, "It's no wonder folks were afraid of him."

"Augustus, pay them no mind," Martha said, as the others laughed, "Welcome to the Lost Jackass Ranch."

"Thank you ma'am, I'm proud to be here."

"It's Martha."

"I beg your pardon."

"It's Martha, not ma'am."

"Yes ma'am...Martha."

After supper, Jace showed Augustus to the bunkhouse. "Take whatever's empty," he said, pointing to the bunks. "But, not that one," he said when Augustus dropped his gear on the nearest empty bunk.

"Something wrong," Augustus asked.

"That was my brother's," Jace said, "He's ah...that is...he's gone."

"What happened to him?"

"We were bushwhacked by the land grabbers one night about a month ago. Tom was the only one that...he was. . . ."

"The dirty son-o-bitches killed him," Haskell said.

"I'm sorry to hear that," Augustus said.

Next morning, just as Tinker was putting breakfast on, Haskell came through the door. "We got all those bodies loaded in the wagon, but they need to be buried."

"How many bodies," Martha asked, getting to her feet.

"You don't want to go out there," Haskell said, blocking the door.

Jace and Augustus soon came in and joined them at the table. "What do you make of those men outside?" Jace asked, "Most of 'em are shot to pieces."

"There was a lot of shooting," Augustus said, "It was pretty bad for a spell."

"That don't explain how you managed to. . . ."

"That's enough," Jonas said interrupting Haskell and putting an end to the morbid conversation, "Eat your breakfast."

"That was mighty good," Augustus said to Tinker when they had finished.

"You're more than welcome," Tinker replied.

"Boy's, it's gonna be a hot day," Jonas said, "We got to get rid of those bodies outside. It isn't likely anybody will be coming for them. I suppose it's up to us, but I don't want them buried anywhere around here."

"What do you proposed to do with them?" Martha asked.

"We didn't invite them here," Jonas said, "They all got what was coming to 'em. We shouldn't have to worry with burying them at all."

"You can't just dump them out somewhere," Martha said.

"I don't see why not," Tinker said, "Coyotes got to eat too."

"You boy's haul 'em at least five miles downwind and bury them all in one big grave," Jonas said.

"One big grave," Clay said, "That will take. . . ."

"Make it deep enough the coyotes can't dig 'em up," Jonas said, "I don't want pieces of them turning up out on the range."

"Come on boys," Clay said, "I guess we got no choice. Let's get it done before they get any riper."

"Come on Augustus," Haskell said, getting to his feet, "You shot most of 'em, you can damn well help bury 'em."

That same morning, Burton Lee was sitting in his new office. He was busy with paper work when Cassidy walked in. "How did it go?" Lee asked.

"I don't rightly know."

"What do you mean?" Lee asked, "Where are the rest of your men?"

"We had the drop on 'em," Cassidy said. "When something…somebody joined in. Jonas must have hired some more men. They were hidden around outside, we didn't see them until it was too late. There must have been a dozen of 'em…shots were coming from everywhere at once. Some of us managed to get away before they got to us, but the rest...I...I need a drink."

Lee produced a bottle from his desk drawer and handed it to Cassidy. The badly shaken gunman pulled the cork and turned it up. Only after several big gulps did he set it down on the desk. "Thanks, I needed that," Cassidy said, wiping his mouth on the back of his hand.

"What now?"

"We're going to need a different kind of gang if we want to get rid of Hobbs."

"What do you mean?"

"I don't know how many guns Hobbs has out there, but it's going to take an army to get at them."

"What are we going to do?"

"I know some boys back in Missouri. They can take care of anything Old Man Hobbs can throw at them."

"Who's that?" Lee asked.

"Sam Cards and some of his kin, they rode with Quantrill in the war, but they been out of work since then. Those Cards boys won't take no for an answer."

"I hate that it's come to this," Lee said, "But after last night, I suppose we have no choice. Get 'em headed this way."

The crew at the Lost Jackass remained on guard for several more nights. There was no sign that any of the surviving raiders were planning on coming back. After a week of quiet nights, Jonas decided it would be safe for them to go to town and stock up on some much needed supplies.

That next morning at breakfast, he began giving out orders. "Jace, I want you and Haskell to move that northern herd back to the valley by Dog Skin Mountain. I think they'll be safe there and we need to take advantage of that grass."

"We'll take care of it," Jace said.

"What about me and Augustus?" Clay asked, "You want us to go with them."

"No," Jonas said, "I want you two to take the buckboard and go to Virginia City. Tinker has a list for you to fill and I need a few things as well. We need a good supply of food and ammunition in case this thing with the railroad isn't over."

"I think I'll ride along with them," Martha said.

"I don't think that's a good idea," Jonas said.

"Why not?"

"Some of that bunch may still be around," Jonas said, "If they see too many of us leave the ranch, they may come back and try to finish what they started the other night."

"I don't believe that for a moment," Martha said, "You just don't want me out there because I'm a woman."

"Either way," Jonas said, "You're not going."

Clay and Augustus made the run to Virginia City and ordered the supplies at the mercantile. Planning on spending the night in town, Clay made arrangements to pick it all up the next morning.

After supper, they made their way to the Brass Rail Saloon. The saloon was busy with quite a few prospectors and townsfolk. Clay ordered a couple of beers and found them a table. Clay was a good looking guy and it wasn't long before he attracted the attention of one of the painted ladies. She came over to their table and took a seat next to Clay.

"I haven't seen you around here before," she said.

"It's been awhile since I was in Virginia City," he replied.

"My name's Tracy Ann and I'm here to show you a good time, if you know what I mean."

"I think I do," Clay said, "But I'm having a good time right here."

While Clay was talking to his newly arrived guest, Augustus began noticing several dust covered, ragged men at another table watching them.

"Hey boy!" one of them shouted across the room. "That's my gal you're a holding there."

"I'm nobody's gal," Tracy Ann shouted back, "least of all some dirt-grubbing Arkansas hillbilly named Francis."

"Dirt-grubbing," Francis said, "You're mine, bought and paid for. Now get your butt back over here!"

"You bought ten minutes worth," Tracy Ann replied. "You done used that up sweet talking me. Course you'd probably only need about a minute to do what you were planning to do." Everybody in the place began to laugh after she said that.

"Is that right," Francis said as he rose to his feet. "I'll show you what can be done in a minute."

"You just sit back down, Francis," Clay said. He really wasn't looking for any part in this argument, but he was caught right in the middle of it.

"You best shut up and stay out of this, Sonny," Francis warned. "Less you want me to teach you a lesson."

"I'm always ready to take a lesson," Clay said, with alcohol induced bravado, "but only from my betters."

The drunken prospector tossed a shot of whiskey into the back of his throat, swallowed it, and wiped his mouth on his dirty sleeve. Several of his friends rose to their feet and started toward Clay's table.

"Are you just gonna sit there?" Clay asked Augustus.

"You jumped into this," Augustus said, "Go on. Show 'em who's the better."

Before Clay could get to his feet, Francis grabbed him by the shirt, yanked him up, and slugged him square in the nose. Clay fell back across the table and rolled onto the floor. Tracy Ann jumped on Francis' back, got him around the neck with her arms, and wrapped her legs around his waist. The drunken prospector was stumbling around and turning a purplish red as she did her best to choke the life out of him.

Clay shook his head, got his legs under him and got to his feet. Francis was still staggering around, trying to get the petticoat wildcat off his back when Clay landed a hard right fist on his face. Tracy Ann was still hanging on as they went to the floor. Two more men went down as Clay slugged one and then the other. Before anyone realized what was happening, one of the prospector's companions came up with a double-barreled shotgun and stuck it in Clay's belly.

The saloon fell silent as Clay froze and slowly raised his hands. The only sound was Augustus' chair as he scooted it back, turning it over behind him. Slowly rising to his feet, he pushed his hat back allowing it to fall onto his shoulders. Pulling back his duster, he exposed both dragoons. "It was just whiskey talking up until now," he warned, "but this has gone far enough. Put down the shotgun and we'll call it even."

"Call it even," Francis said, struggling to his feet, "You got a one sided view of even, Mister."

"Maybe so," Augustus said, "The boy was just showing off for the lady. There's no shortage of loose women in this town, I'm sure you can find plenty more where this one came from. There's no need for anyone to die in here tonight."

"Thanks a lot," Tracy Ann said, getting back to her feet.

"Mister, I think you're a coward," Francis said to Augustus, "Too scared to fight fair."

"I'm gonna cut this boy in half if I pull this trigger," the man with the shotgun warned.

"Go ahead, Buck," Francis said, "kill him. This coward ain't gonna do. . . ."

"If you do," Augustus warned, never taking his eyes off Buck, "I'll kill you and every man with you."

"Big talk," Francis said, "There's five of us."

"All five of you will die, but Buck will be first."

"Suppose we kill you first?" Francis asked.

"You won't kill me," Augustus said, "But that won't keep me from killing all of you."

"The hell we won't," Francis repeated, "Go ahead, Buck, show him."

All the while Francis was running his mouth, Buck was watching Augustus' eyes. He saw something there that frightened him and he lost his nerve. "Shut up, Francis," Buck said, still watching Augustus. Pulling back, he lowered his shotgun, and let the hammers down, "I'm not sure what he is, but this man is no coward."

"Don't let that half-breed buffalo you," Francis said to Buck, "Kill him."

"If you want him dead, kill him yourself," Buck said, all the while watching Augustus, "The man's right, we're all a little drunk. We was just funning…no reason to…no need for any killing." Never taking his eyes from Augustus, Buck stepped around Clay and made his way to the door. His companions took hold of Francis and followed Buck out the door without any further words.

Augustus closed his coat when they were gone and picked his chair up from the floor. He pulled it back up to their table and took a seat.

"You can be pretty damn scary when you want to be," Clay said, picking up his hat.

"I suppose," Augustus said with a grin.

"You would've killed every one of them, if they hadn't backed down."

"Just as sure as you're sitting there."

They loaded the wagon next morning and set out for home. It was afternoon when they crossed the Truckee River and spotted the Red Dog Saloon. "How about a drink," Clay asked.

"I think you had enough to drink last night," Augustus said.

"That was last night," Clay said with a grin, "This is today and I'm thirsty."

"All right," Augustus said, "I might just have one."

Leaving the wagon in the street, they went in the saloon, found a table and spent an hour having a bite to eat and a few beers. After draining his third mug, Clay was in the mood to talk. "I was too drunk to think about it much last night," he said. "What did you mean when you told those men they wouldn't kill you?"

"I think we need to get on to the ranch, before it gets dark," Augustus said getting to his feet.

"Yeah, I guess you're right."

Cassidy was just coming out of Lee's office when he spotted Clay and Augustus. He ran back in and motioned for the rest of his men to join him. The six of them walked up the street to start a confrontation. Burton Lee was watching from his office window.

"What are you boy's doing in Reno?" Cassidy asked.

Turning around, Clay recognized Cassidy. "That's none of your business," he said.

72

"Suppose I make it my business?" Cassidy asked, "What's in the wagon?"

Augustus walked to the rear of the wagon and stood on Clay's right, "Like the man said, it's none of your business."

"I heard him," Cassidy said as he studied Augustus, "That's one butt-ugly hat you got there on your head. Where'd . . . ."

"I don't think you're in a position to call anything butt-ugly," Augustus said, before Cassidy could finish.

"You got a real smart mouth on you, Stranger," Cassidy said, as Clay began to laugh, "Do them old fashion horse pistols of yours still shoot?"

"One way to find out," Augustus said, pushing his hat back and allowing it to fall onto his shoulders.

While Cassidy was talking, the men with him spread out to the sides. Each of them was armed with a rifle. Seeing the confrontation in the street, several bystanders gathered to watch the showdown. Burton Lee hurried up the sidewalk to join them.

"Didn't you learn anything the other night?" Clay asked.

"I don't know what you're talking about," Cassidy said.

"You're a liar," Clay said.

"Nobody calls me a liar and lives, Boy," Cassidy said. He could see Clay was unarmed. "You need to start apologizing before I. . . ."

"I say, you're a liar and a coward," Clay said, "I saw you turn tail and run when the shooting started."

Cassidy's face flushed blood red, "I never turned tail from anybody. What about you, Horse Pistols," he asked looking back to Augustus, "You gonna do this boy's fighting for him?"

"If need be."

"There's too many of 'em," Clay whispered to Augustus, "We need to go."

"Too late for that," Augustus said, still watching Cassidy.

"Is Old Man Hobbs paying you enough to get yourself killed over this boy?" Cassidy asked.

"You won't kill me," Augustus warned, "But that won't keep me from killing all of you."

"We won't kill you," Cassidy repeated, "I guess we'll just have to see about. . . ." as he spoke, Cassidy went for his gun. His already doomed companions foolishly followed his lead.

Augustus pulled a dragoon with his right hand, firing a shot at Cassidy, while he pulled Clay down behind him with his left. Cassidy was spun violently backwards as his leg was knocked out from under him by Augustus' first bullet.

With Clay safely out of the way, Augustus pulled the other dragoon. The bystanders ducked as the street was suddenly filled with deafening gunshots and billowing clouds of smoke from the black powder. Even in the midst of all the chaos, Augustus stood calm and steady. Smoke and fire belched from the dragoons as he methodically cocked and fired each one. One gunman after another was hit and driven backwards with the impact of the heavy bullets.

Clay was clinging to the ground and covering his ears as multiple bullets slammed into the wagon bed over his head. The gunfight only lasted a few moments. When it was nearly over, the last man standing lost his nerve and turned to flee. Without hesitation, Augustus raised the dragoon in his right hand and put a bullet between the coward's shoulder blades, driving him into the dirt.

Cassidy was down and bleeding from a bullet in his thigh, but still alive. His five companions were all dead. Augustus was still on his feet and untouched.

"Are you all right?" Augustus asked, holstering the dragoons and helping Clay to his feet.

"Yeah," he said, "I…ah…how did you…that was something."

"I think you better start wearing a gun."

"It's in the wagon," Clay said, "But, I think you may be right."

Augustus walked over to where Cassidy lay and spoke to him. "That's twice you've managed to live through a gun fight with me. For your sake, there had better not be another."

"The second," Cassidy said. "So you're one of the hidden gunmen from Hobbs' place."

"I thought you didn't know anything about that?"

"Wait a minute…I…I know you," Cassidy said. He suddenly remembered the twin dragoons and realized he had seen the piercing dark eyes and the raven black hair of the gunman standing over him before, "I do know you...you...you gave me this," he said pointing to his scar. "You don't remember me, do you?"

"Stay away from the Hobbs' family," Augustus said without answering. While the stunned crowd watched, he put his boot in the middle of Cassidy's chest, pinning him to the ground. Holstering the gun in his left hand, Augustus bent down and pressed the muzzle of the other dragoon against Cassidy's forehead. The crowd on the sidewalk remained silent. None of them wanted any part of the dark and deadly gunman holding Cassidy down.

Cassidy began to tremble as he watched the changes come over Augustus. The normally strong voice grew deeper and hollow. The intense dark eyes shone a dull yellow with narrow ebony slits for pupils as he stared intently into Cassidy's face.

In the strained silence of the street, it sounded as if Augustus was unlocking the gates of hell when he placed his thumb on the hammer of the dragoon and cocked it, "Charlie Nighthorse was a friend of mine," he whispered, "If I find out you had anything to do with murdering his family, I'll be back to kill you, and no power on earth can keep me from it."

Leaving Cassidy lying limp and bloody in the street, Augustus holstered his gun and walked away. He climbed up in the wagon seat beside Clay and headed the team out of town. None of the townsfolk tried to stop them as they drove away.

"Did you see his eyes?" one of the men standing beside Burton Lee asked.

"Take Cassidy to my office," Lee said, without answering, "Some of you men get these bodies off the street."

Just at sundown, two days later, Jace and Haskell rode in from Dog Skin Mountain. "Where have you all been?" Jonas asked. "We expected you back this morning."

"We rode down to that new town by the river," Haskell said.

"We heard there was a saloon," Jace said, "wanted to see what all the fuss is about."

"You made a pretty big impression," Haskell said to Augustus.

75

"What do you mean?" Jonas asked, before Augustus could answer. .

"Clay and the Kid here were at the Red Dog Saloon in Reno the other day," Jace said.

"How come I haven't heard about that?" Jonas asked, turning to Clay, "You were supposed to be in Virginia City."

"We were," Clay said, "We stopped for a bite to eat and a beer on the way back."

"What happened," Jonas asked turning back to Jace, "and who's the Kid?"

"That's what they're calling him in town," Haskell said, "The Reno Kid. Townsfolk claim they never saw such a cold-blooded gunfighter."

"Gunfighter," Jonas repeated, "Who's a gunfighter?"

"He took on half-a-dozen men, Cassidy was one of them," Jace said, "The Kid was protecting Clay when he shot Cassidy in the leg. Bullets were flying all around him, when he shot the others...dead!"

"Dead as canned corned beef!" Haskell said, "Every damn one of 'em!"

"The Kid never got a scratch," Jace said.

"Not one scratch," Haskell repeated, "The wagon's shot to pieces, but not the Kid. Some of the witnesses claim he's bullet proof."

"That railroad man, Burton Lee, wanted the law to come up here and get him," Jace said, "but a dozen witnesses say it was a fair fight, and Cassidy started it."

"But the Kid damn sure finished it," Haskell said, "he damn sure did!"

"Who's the Kid?" Jonas demanded.

"Augustus," Haskell said, "The Reno Kid, that's what they're calling him. Every town needs a legend, now Reno's got a humdinger!"

"Well I'll be damned," Jonas said. "Where were you when this was happening?" he asked, turning to Clay.

"I was on the ground. Augustus...the Kid, pulled me down out of the way while he was shooting at Cassidy. That's the only reason, Cassidy's still alive."

"Why did Augustus have to pull you out of the way?" Martha asked.

"I ah...I wasn't wearing my gun," Clay said, "It was in the wagon."

"I guess you saved my son's life," Jonas said to Augustus.

"It was nothing," Augustus said, "It all happened pretty fast. I'm just sorry I didn't kill Cassidy when I had the chance."

"It was much more than nothing," Martha said, "We're mighty grateful. The Reno Kid," she said, taking his hand, "I like that."

Augustus was in the barn that night after supper, when Martha walked in. "What are you up to?" she asked.

"Just cleaning my saddle," Augustus replied.

"It's a nice saddle, Mexican isn't it?"

"Yeah, I got it when I was working over in California. Half the cowboys there were Mexican."

"Were there any Mexican ladies in California?"

"A few, why do you. . . ."

"Have you ever been in love?"

Augustus was taken back for a moment, not sure how they went from saddles to his love life. "Well, I can't say that I have," he said.

"Certainly, a man like you has been with a woman."

"Yes," he said, "I've been with several women over the years, but it was never anything I would call love."

"Surely you loved somebody in your life," she asked, moving closer to him.

"I remember that I loved my mother," he said, "but I've never been in love with anyone."

"That's hard for me to believe."

"Ms. Martha," he said, "maybe this is something we shouldn't be talking about in here. Some of the boys might come in and I wouldn't want them to get the wrong idea."

"Nobody is around, we're alone, stop worrying."

"How about you," he asked, trying to get her focus off of him, "You ever been in love?"

"Love...I suppose. There have been a few men in my life, but nothing serious and none lately."

"You're a handsome woman. I'm sure the right one will come along."

"You don't have to lie. I know I'm plain looking," she said, "There's no need to flatter me, but I'm a woman and as a woman, I have needs, if you know what I mean."

"I believe I do," he said, "But I don't know what that has to do with me."

"I'm about to show you, Reno," she said, unbuttoning the front of her shirt. "It's alright if I call you Reno, isn't it? You do like women don't you?"

"As much as any other man, I suppose. You can call me anything you like, but Martha, you should know before this happens, I won't, I can't fall in love with you."

"Nobody is talking about love," she said. "Right now, we're talking about needs."

Augustus' bedroll was still tied behind his saddle. Martha loosened the bedroll and led him back to a stall stacked with hay. She spread the bedroll out on a bed of hay and lay down on it, motioning for Augustus to join her.

When he was beside her, Martha pressed her mouth to his and began unbuckling his belt. Making love to the boss' daughter wasn't anything Augustus had planned, but it was way too late to stop at that point.

While eagerly returning the kisses she was giving him, Augustus helped her out of her pants. When she was finally free of her manly clothes, Martha was remarkably feminine and sensuous. Overcoming their initial awkwardness, they soon became comfortable and familiar with each other's body. Martha was an aggressive and strong-willed woman. She knew exactly what she wanted from Augustus and she knew how to get it. They made love for nearly an hour until they were both exhausted.

"Now, that wasn't so bad, was it?" she asked as she lay next to him.

"I thought all along you were a tomboy," Augustus said.

"I can be when I want to be."

"I can believe that," he said.

Martha was feeling playful and after spying Augustus' hat, she stood up and plucked it off the hay stack. Wearing nothing but a big smile, she put it on and turned back to Augustus, "How do I look?"

Standing there buck-naked under the big sombrero, it was difficult to find any fault with how she looked. "You ah…you look just like a real bandito," Augustus said, "about the best looking one I ever saw, as a matter of fact."

Still wearing the hat, Martha came back to Augustus' side. "What's this," she asked examining the amulet around Augustus' neck.

"My mother gave it to me the day she died," he said, "Belonged to my father. It's pretty old."

"It's beautiful," she said. "Do you always wear it?"

"Always," I think it saved my life once."

"When was that?"

"It's a long story, maybe later."

"All right then. Tell me more about this problem you have with love. Not that I care one way or the other, mind you. I'm just curious."

"I wouldn't call it a problem. It's just after that night at Pyramid Lake; I haven't felt much of anything as far as emotion goes."

"What happened at Pyramid Lake?"

Augustus realized he had let his guard down and had already said too much, "Nothing really, it was a long time ago."

"Is that where you got this scar?"

"As a matter of fact, it is, but it's a long story. You wouldn't believe me if I told you. There are times when I don't even believe it."

"I care about you," she said, "I'll believe anything you tell me. Maybe it would help to talk about it."

"If you do care about me, don't ask. Just believe me when I say that I can't love you. Not that I don't want to, I just can't. I have obligations and I don't know when I'll be called upon to fulfill them. I could be gone tomorrow and never see you again."

"In that case," she said getting to her feet and dropping the hat, "I'll just say goodnight."

"Martha, wait. I didn't mean to hurt you."

"I'm not hurt," she said, gathering up her clothes, "This was about needs, nothing more, goodnight."

Chapter Seven: Kidnapped

It was a week later when Burton Lee saw six men ride up, tie their horses, and enter the Red Dog. "Who do you suppose that is?" he asked Cassidy.

Turning to peer out the window, Cassidy began to smile, "The men we've been waiting for," he said, "Come on."

Cassidy was still using a crutch to get around. He was hurrying as best he could to make his way up the street. "Sam, Sam Cards!" he shouted upon entering the Red Dog.

"Well, I'll be damned," the big man at the bar said when he spotted Cassidy, "You are still alive."

"What do you mean?" Cassidy asked.

"Your missus told everybody back home that you were killed by Indians years ago."

"Why would she do something like that?"

"Probably so she could marry the blacksmith," Cards said, "I suppose a woman could get lonely after ten years of sleeping by herself."

"I suppose," Cassidy agreed, "but Tolliver, she married Tolliver?"

"She sure did," Cards said, "They lit out for California right after the ceremony."

"What about my boys?"

"They went with her of course."

"Well, I...ah...reckon they're better off."

"I reckon," Cards agreed, "What happened to you?"

"Had a little fight with the Reno Kid, you might say he got lucky."

"I'd say luck had little to do with it," Lee said.

"The Reno Kid," Cards said, "Don't believe I've heard of him."

"From what I've seen and heard, you'd do well to stay clear of him," Lee said.

"He's a hired gun that works for the people we want you to get rid of," Cassidy said. "This is Burton Lee, our boss."

"Mr. Lee," Cards said, "Sam Cards. This here's my kid brother, Timmy. It's good to meet you."

"Likewise," Lee said, "I thought you'd have more men."

"Things are tough back in Missouri," Sam said, "There ain't many of us left. Don't you worry, Mr. Lee, there's enough of us to get this job done."

"Let's find a table so I can take a load off," Cassidy said, "I'll tell you all about our problem."

Cassidy spent several minutes explaining why he had sent for Cards and his men. "The way I see it," Sam said, "The only way to get the right-of-way is to kill off the Hobbs' clan."

"That's about the size of it," Cassidy said.

"We've tried everything else," Lee said. "There are important people involved in this, not to mention a fortune to be made after the railroad is finished. The people in Carson City want this matter put to bed right away. We need to notify the railroad they can begin laying track as soon as they break through the Sierras."

"Why don't you and your boys ride out there tonight and finish it?" Cassidy asked.

"Not a chance," Sam said, "You already tried that. No sense in getting my men killed trying to flush them out of that house."

"So, what's your plan?" Lee asked.

"We need to lay low," Sam said. "We'll hide out in the hills until we can catch some of them out alone. If we can kill a few of them, the rest will come after you here in town and we can finish it on our own ground."

"There's one more thing you need to know," Cassidy said. "That half-breed gunfighter that works for Hobbs, the one they're calling the Reno Kid, he's ah...he's different."

"What do you mean, different?" Timmy asked.

"He's dangerous, real dangerous," Cassidy said, "He has long black hair like an Indian, wears a big slouchy sombrero, and he carries a set of Colt Dragoons. He don't scare worth a damn, and he's got cold eyes, almost as if. . . ."

"You're scared of him," Sam said.

"Damn right, I am. You will be too, if you face him," Cassidy warned, "I've known him for a long time. He very nearly killed me twice. Don't give him a chance to defend himself; you likely won't live through it."

Three days later, Martha, Jace, and Haskell were in the valley below Dog Skin Mountain checking cattle. The day was winding down and they decided to take the road back toward the house. They had only traveled a short distance when Jace spotted six riders coming across the sagebrush from the west. "We got company," he said.

"Who is it?" Haskell asked.

"Don't believe I know 'em," Jace said.

"Howdy folks," the big man said when he rode up.

"Howdy yourself," Haskell said, "What are you men doing way up here?"

"Trying to earn a dollar," Cards said.

"What kind of work do you do?" Martha asked, "Mr. . . ."

"Cards, Ma'am," the stranger said, removing his hat, "Sam Cards, from Missouri."

"You're a long way from Missouri," Haskell said.

"That's a fact," Sam said.

Haskell was becoming uneasy after noticing the stranger was covering his holster with the hat. "Ms. Martha," he said, "we need to. . . ."

"I don't believe you said why you're out here," Martha said.

"I beg your pardon," Sam said, "Truth is Ma'am, we're here for you."

Before Jace or Haskell could react, several shots were fired from the Cards brothers and their men. Both of them were shot before they ever got their guns out of the holster. Martha tried to pull her rifle, but Sam stopped her. "I wouldn't do that if I were you," he warned.

Martha sat quiet as six men held their guns on her. Timmy Cards dismounted and tied her hands to her saddle horn. "Where are we taking her?" Timmy asked.

Cassidy says there are plenty of old mining shacks over in the mountains," Sam said.

"Cassidy!" Martha declared, "That son-of-a-bitch!"

"Yes Ma'am," Sam replied with a grin. "Me and Carrot Top are going back to Reno," he said to Timmy, "You all take her to the mountains and find a good place to hide her. After you get her hidden away, leave a couple of the boys to watch her. You get back to Reno and let us know where she is."

"We'll do that," Timmy said. Climbing back on his horse, he gathered up Martha's reins.

"And Timmy, Boy," Sam said, "I don't want her damaged, if you know what I mean."

"We'll take good care of her."

"I mean it, Timmy," Sam repeated, "She's a lady."

"All right...all right," Timmy said.

Sam and Carrot Top headed back to Reno, while Timmy and three others headed out cross country toward the west. Before he got on his horse, Sam stuffed an envelope under Jace's vest.

It was long after dark when Jonas began to think something was bad wrong. "Where do you suppose they are?" he asked Tinker. "I knew I shouldn't have let her go with them."

"They should have been here by now," Tinker replied.

"Me and Augustus will go look for them," Clay said.

"I'm going with you," Jonas said, "They were supposed to be in the valley below Dog Skin this afternoon."

They had only gone about a mile when they met Jace and Haskell's horses on the road. "This ain't good," Jonas said.

"There's blood here," Augustus said examining Haskell's saddle.

"Come on," Jonas said, "Bring those horses. We may need 'em." After another five miles, they found Jace and Haskell still lying in the road where they fell. Jonas was frantically searching the brush around them, but there was no sign of Martha or her horse.

It was obvious to Clay and Augustus that Jace was gone. The bullet had entered dead center of his chest and shredded his heart. He was probably dead before he hit the ground. When they rolled Haskell over, he groaned.

"Haskell's still alive," Clay said.

"Haskell," Jonas said, reaching their side, "Where's Martha? What happened to Martha?"

"They...took her," Haskell whispered.

"Took her," Jonas repeated, "Who took her?"

"Strangers...man named. . . ."

"A man named what?" Jonas demanded.

"Easy Pa," Clay said, "Let him talk."

"Cards," Haskell said, "Sam Cards, said he was from Missouri."

"Did he say why they took her?" Augustus asked.

"No...but...but Cassidy told them to."

"Cassidy," Jonas repeated, "I'm gonna kill him for this."

"We're going to kill all of them," Augustus said, "But first we have to get Haskell to a doctor and we have to find Martha."

"Clay, you ride for the ranch," Jonas said, "Get the buckboard and Tinker, and get back here as fast as you can. You get Haskell to the doctor in Virginia City. Me and Augustus are going after Martha."

"You hold on, Haskell," Clay said when he was in the saddle, "I'll be right back." With that, he turned his horse and spurred him away into the night.

"Can you remember anything else?" Augustus asked Haskell.

"I seem to remember them saying something about an old claim over in the mountains. Where's Jace...is he. . . ."

"He's gone," Jonas said.

"First Tom and now Jace," Haskell said, "Kid, are you there?"

"I'm here," Augustus replied, taking Haskell's hand.

"You got to get them sons-o-bitches for me and Jace."

"I'm going to get all of them," Augustus said, "And you're going to help me."

"I'm done for," Haskell said, "I ain't bulletproof like you."

"You're not dead yet," Augustus said, examining Haskell's wound, "You were lucky."

"Yeah, that's me," Haskell said, "If you call lying here in this damn road, bleeding to death, lucky?"

"The bullet went clear through, you ornery old croaker," Augustus said, "I don't know how, but your lungs are clear and your heart's still pumping. If you don't go and quit on me, you should pull through."

"I ain't quitting on nobody," Haskell said, "You can bet your saddle on that."

"All right then," Augustus said, "Let's get some pressure on that wound. That ought to hold you till Clay can get you to the doctor."

Clay and Tinker were back in just over an hour. They got Haskell loaded into the buckboard and headed out toward Virginia City.

"What are we gonna do now?" Jonas asked.

"First, we'll take Jace home and bury him," Augustus said, "It'll be daylight by the time we get that done and get back here."

"What's that?" Jonas asked, spying the envelope that had fallen out when they laid Jace's body across his saddle.

"It's addressed to you," Augustus said, handing it to Jonas.

Jonas opened the blood-stained envelope and unfolded the letter inside. "What's it say," Augustus asked.

"When I sign this release for the right-of-way, and deliver it to Burton Lee, we get Martha back."

"How do they think they can get away with that?" Augustus said. "That release won't be worth the paper it's printed on when the law finds out how they got it."

"I'm sure as soon as they get this release in hand, they're planning on killing all of us before we can tell anybody about it," Jonas said, "I don't believe we'll ever see Martha again if we don't find her ourselves."

"We're going to find Martha," Augustus said, "When she's safe, we'll hunt them all down, Lee, Cassidy, and this Sam Cards, whoever he is."

"Can you track those men who have Martha?"

"I'm going to try," Augustus said. "It seems one group went south toward Reno. Another group went west toward the mountains."

"I doubt if they were bold enough to take her to town."

"I'd say you're right about that," Augustus said, "I say she's with the bunch headed toward the mountains. Beckwourth taught me about tracking and I know the Sierras pretty well, I say we go after them."

"We'll leave Clay a note at the ranch and let him know where we're going."

It was sundown, two days later, when Timmy Cards rolled out his bedroll and sat down by their campfire. "Well, Ms. Martha," he said, "This seems like a nice place. We should be real comfortable here." They were camped near an old abandoned claim shack just above the Feather River. "You can take the shack. Me and the boys will stay out here."

"Just what do you plan to do with me?" Martha asked.

"Me," Timmy said, "I ain't planning to do nothing with you."

"Then why am I here?"

"As soon as your daddy signs away that right-of-way, you can go home."

"So this is about the railroad?"

"It seems so," Timmy said.

"Suppose you just let me go and my daddy will pay you for your trouble?"

"If it was just up to me, Ma'am, I'd say that would be fine."

"But it's not up to you?"

"That's a fact," Timmy said, "My big brother, Sam, is running this outfit. He's done right well by me so far and I ain't gonna buck him."

"How long are we going to be here?"

"That depends on your old man."

"How will we know when to go?"

"You sure do ask a lot of fool questions. I'm headed back to Reno in the morning. I'll come back for you when Sam gets that signed release from your daddy."

"I hate to be the one to break this to you, Timmy," Martha said, "But that ain't going to happen. My daddy won't ever sign that paper, and he'll hunt you down and kill you for this."

"I know you believe that, but we got plenty of men to handle anything your daddy can throw against us."

"Timmy, believe me when I tell you, my daddy ain't the only one that's going to be throwing."

87

"We ain't scared of your little brother, if that's who you mean, nor that Reno Kid feller, whoever he is."

"Well, you've been warned."

"Hello in the camp!" a voice shouted from the darkness. Augustus and Jonas were camped beside the Feather River and having a bite to eat.

"That sounds like Clay," Jonas said.

"Come on in," Augustus shouted, "but come easy till we can see your face!"

"Say," Clay said when he could see them by the fire, "aren't you the famous Reno Kid?"

"That's me," Augustus said, "Protector of the drunk and unarmed."

"I wasn't drunk," Clay said getting down from his horse."

"You made good time catching up with us," Jonas said, "How's Haskell."

"Doc says he'll live, but he's gonna be laid up awhile. I left him and Tinker in Virginia City."

"They'll be safer there than at the ranch all alone," Augustus said.

"Any sign of Martha?" Clay asked.

"Not yet," Augustus said, "But we're getting close."

"Why do you say that?"

"Cards' men aren't going to cross the mountains with her. There's no reason to go to all that trouble. They're hiding her along this river, unless I miss my guess."

"Get some rest, Clay," Jonas said, "we're out of here at first light."

It was just after nine the next morning when Augustus held up his hand for silence. "What is it?" Clay asked when he rode up beside him.

"I smell smoke," Augustus said. "Somebody is camped up ahead there."

"What are we gonna do?"

"Cards and his men don't know me," Augustus said, "I'm going to ride up there nice and friendly and find out who they are."

"What do you want us to do?" Jonas asked.

"You two move up through the trees and get around behind them. I'll give you time to get there."

"Sounds like a good plan," Clay said.

"Just remember," Augustus warned, "They may be just harmless settlers. We don't want to shoot any innocent people."

"There's somebody coming," one of Timmy's men warned when he spotted Augustus.

"Where?" Timmy asked.

"Down the river there, one man on horseback, looks like a Mexican." A slight smile crossed Martha's lips when the kidnapper mentioned a Mexican.

"Probably nothing," Timmy said, "But get her inside and keep her quiet."

One of the gunmen helped Martha up and pushed her toward the cabin. When they were inside, the gunman forced her to the floor under the only window. Her hands were still tied, and he pulled off his neckerchief and bound it around her mouth to silence her. After she was secure, he took up a position at the window. The nervous kidnapper held his gun at her head while he peered through the dirty glass.

Timmy and his other men were sitting by the fire when Augustus rode up. "Morning," Augustus said, "Coffee smells good."

"We got none to spare," Timmy said, "What are you doing on our claim?"

"Just passing through, smelled your smoke. What kind of claim is this?" Augustus asked, looking around, "I thought the gold played out around here long ago." While he was speaking, Augustus noticed the nervous man at the window.

The long haired stranger was jogging Timmy's memory, but he couldn't recall why he seemed familiar. "What we're doing here ain't no concern to some damn Mexican half-breed," Timmy said, "Now move on before we have to do something you'll regret."

"I'll be going," Augustus said, pulling back his coat.

"Where'd you get that horse?" one of Timmy's companions asked. "That's a fine animal, too good for a Mexican or an Indian, or whatever kind of cur-dog you are." The mouthy gunman worked the lever on the rifle he was holding as he continued to taunt Augustus, "If you stay around here much longer, Poncho, I might just have to take him away from you."

Augustus pushed his hat back and let it fall between his shoulders, "Before you do that," he said with a smile, "I want to know if you boys have seen anything of Martha Hobbs, attractive lady, mid-thirties, rides the horse you got hidden out. . . ."

Suddenly remembering Cassidy's warning, Timmy pulled his pistol. The men at the fire followed his lead and went for their guns. Augustus pulled his pistols and fired the first shot through the window. Martha was showered with broken glass as her kidnapper was driven back against the opposite wall.

Timmy got off one hurried shot before he took a bullet from Augustus. The third kidnapper got off two shots before he was killed by Augustus. The man who threatened to take Augustus' horse dropped his rifle and tried to make a run for it. Augustus shot him in the back of the head, splattering his brains all over the ground.

"I thought you were gonna wait for us," Clay said as he rode in and bailed off his horse.

"Where's Martha?" Jonas asked when he joined them.

"Inside, I believe," Augustus said, stepping down from his horse.

Without trying the latch, Jonas burst through the door with his shoulder and found Martha lying on the floor. "Are you all right?" he asked as he knelt beside her. The gunman that had been guarding her was lying against the far wall with his eyes locked in a ghoulish stare and a neat round hole in the middle of his forehead.

"I'm fine," she said, when the gag was off, "It's about damn time you all got here." In spite of her brave act, after getting to her feet, Martha put her arms around her father and held him tight. "How did you know I was in here?" she asked turning to Augustus.

"I knew as soon as I rode up, this bunch wasn't prospecting," Augustus said, "These claims were abandoned years ago and they didn't have any tools lying around anywhere. The nervous one in the window gave it away."

"That's the second time you've saved one of my children," Jonas said.

"Yeah," Augustus said, "You raised a pretty wild bunch."

"I'm mighty tired of dealing with this Burton Lee and his henchman," Jonas said.

"I think you're right," Augustus said, "It's time to finish this."

Chapter Eight: The Hanging

It was late in the evening when Augustus and the Hobbs' clan rode into Reno. Burton Lee's office was closed up and dark. "They're probably in the saloon," Clay said.

"You stay out here," Jonas said to Martha.

"Sorry," she said, pulling her rifle, "I owe this bunch."

Sam Cards was sitting with four men playing poker and having a drink when he looked up and saw Martha walk through the door. All the blood drained from his face when the other men came in behind her. From what he had heard, he was pretty sure the older man was Jonas Hobbs and the big half-breed with the long black hair was the Reno Kid.

Before Sam could decide what to do, Martha worked the lever on her rifle and pointed it at his chest. Recognizing Augustus, everyone in the place, except for the men sitting with Sam, got up and headed for the door.

"What's the meaning of all this?" Cards asked.

"You can drop the act," Martha said, "Everyone here knows what you are."

"The rest of you just sit real still if you want to live through this," Clay said holding his gun on the men at the table.

"Where's Burton Lee and Cassidy?" Jonas asked.

"Gone," Sam said.

"Gone where?"

"Carson City, to see the Governor."

"I don't know who you people are," one of the men at the table said, "But we ain't part of this. We just sat down here to play poker."

"Did you ever see these men?" Jonas asked Martha.

"Not these two here," she said, "But Carrot Top there is the one that shot Haskell."

"All right," Augustus said, "You two can go, but I wouldn't hang around here long."

"Don't worry, Mister," one of them said gathering up his winnings, "we're getting out of here right now."

"You two get up," Augustus said, after the gamblers were gone.

"What are you gonna do?" Sam asked.

"Aren't you even slightly interested in what happened to your brother?" Martha asked.

"I figured, since you're here and he ain't. . . ."

"You figured right," Clay said. "He made the mistake of drawing on the Reno Kid."

"I guess that would be you," Cards said looking at Augustus.

"Seems like," Augustus said.

"Well you don't impress me, Mister Reno Kid, and I'm gonna kill you for shooting my little brother."

"Just exactly how do you plan to do that?" Clay asked.

"I'll find a way," Sam said.

"In the mean time, you're coming with us," Augustus said.

"Where to," Sam asked.

"Carson City," Jonas said, "You're gonna tell the marshal who put you up to kidnapping my daughter and killing my cowhands."

"Suppose I won't?"

"You will," Augustus said. Grabbing Cards by the collar, Augustus yanked him out his seat and shoved him toward the door.

Early the next morning, Burton Lee and Cassidy were at the Governor's Mansion in Carson City. "What brings you around," Governor Maxwell asked.

"We just wanted to let you know that we should have the deed to Jonas Hobbs' place in the next day or so," Lee said

"One of our men will be along with it anytime now," Cassidy said.

"That sounds like great news," Maxwell said, "But you fools are just a little too late."

"What do you mean?" Lee asked.

"While you were out fooling around with Jonas Hobbs, the Central Pacific changed the route. It's going thirty miles north of their first survey."

"They can't do that," Lee said, "Not after all I've been. . . ."

"They can and they have," Maxwell said, "You have lost a fortune."

"Me," Lee said, "You mean us."

"The railroad is still in Nevada," Maxwell said, "and I'm still governor. I'll get my share."

"That damn Reno Kid is to blame for all of this," Cassidy said, "This would have been over long ago if he hadn't showed up."

"He'll pay for his meddling," Lee said.

"From what I hear," Maxwell said, "You would do well to leave him alone."

"I think I know how we can get at that half-breed," Cassidy said.

"How's that," Maxwell asked.

"He was with Numaga when Ormsby's Militia was ambushed and murdered," Cassidy said.

"How could you possibly know that?" Lee asked.

"I was at the William's Station in May of '60 and I was with Ormsby a week later when we were ambushed," Cassidy said.

"And you saw the Reno Kid with the Indians?" Lee asked.

"Saw him," Cassidy said, "We were face to face. He's the one that gave me this eye. He was dressed like an Indian, but he was carrying those twin dragoons and he had a round scar right in the middle of his chest. I'd recognize that scar if I ever see it again."

Maxwell sent his clerk down the street to get Marshal Webster. "Yes Sir," Webster asked when he arrived, "What can I do for you?"

"You've heard of the man known as the Reno Kid?" Maxwell asked.

"Yes Sir, most of it is hard to believe though."

"I want a warrant issued for him right away."

"Mr. Lee already tried that," Webster said, "Too many witnesses took the Kid's side."

"This is different," Maxwell said. He went on to explain what Cassidy had told him.

"What do you want him charged with?" Webster asked.

"Multiple counts of murder," Maxwell said, "You'll have to ride to Jonas Hobbs' ranch to find him."

"Jonas Hobbs and his daughter are in my office right now," Webster said.

"What are they doing here?" Lee asked.

"Swearing out warrants against a man named Sam Cards and his partner for kidnapping Ms. Hobbs."

"How in hell did they…where is Cards?" Cassidy asked.

"In one of my cells, Clay Hobbs and one of their hired hands brought them in at gunpoint."

"This hired hand," Cassidy asked, "Big man, sombrero, twin revolvers, long black hair?"

"That's him," Webster said.

"That's the Reno Kid," Cassidy said.

"The Reno Kid is here?" Maxwell said, suddenly out of his chair, "This…ah…this could be bad. We have to be careful until he's safely locked up. We need a plan, Webster. I don't want a blood bath in the streets, and I damn sure don't want him coming up here."

Jonas and Martha were just finishing up their statements when Marshal Webster returned. "Are you about done?" he asked. The marshal seemed to be on edge as he walked behind his desk.

"I believe that's got it," Jonas said.

"Those two men outside," Webster asked, "Were they witnesses to any of this?"

"Yes they were," Martha said.

"Ask them to step in here for just a moment, if you don't mind."

"There's just one thing," Jonas said.

"And that would be what?" Webster asked.

"We hear that Cassidy is right here in Carson City. Why isn't he in your jail?"

"Believe me, Mr. Hobbs. If Cassidy was in Carson City, I would know about it. Now would you please get those men outside?"

"What do you need, Marshal?" Clay asked when they were inside.

"I just want to ask you boys a couple of questions," Webster said, turning to the rack of firearms behind him. Suddenly reaching for a double-barreled shotgun, he pulled it down and pointed at Martha. As soon as he did, two more deputies stormed in the door.

"What the hell?" Jonas asked.

"All right, Kid," Webster said to Augustus, "Just be real still and none of these people will have to die."

Augustus knew if he pulled a gun, Webster would kill Martha. "Put your gun on the desk," Webster said to Clay. The young Hobbs did as he was told, "All right," Webster said to Clay, "Just ease those pistols out of the Kid's holsters and put 'em on the desk."

When Augustus was disarmed, Webster ordered him into a cell. Only after locking the cell door did Webster take a deep breath and wipe the sweat from his brow. "Tell them they can come in now," he said to one of his deputies.

Jonas was surprised when Burton Lee, Cassidy, and the Governor walked in. "What's the meaning of this?" he demanded of Webster. "I thought you said Cassidy wasn't in Carson City."

"Cassidy was with Mr. Lee in Reno on the night of that shooting," Governor Maxwell said, "The charges have been dropped."

"You're a lying two-faced son-of-a-bitch!" Jonas declared.

"Marshal," Maxwell said turning away from Jonas, "Would you please just serve the warrant."

"What are the charges?" Martha asked.

"Murder," Cassidy said, "This man you all think so highly of was with Numaga and those Paiute murderers when they slaughtered Major Ormsby and the militia."

"That's ridiculous," Martha said, "What proof do you have?"

"I was there," Cassidy said, "He very nearly killed me with a club."

"It's your word against his," Jonas said.

"I can prove what I'm saying is true," Cassidy said, "The Indian that attacked me was wearing those big horse pistols and he had a big round scar, right in the middle of his chest." Martha's face paled when Cassidy said that.

"Is any of this true?" Jonas asked, turning to Augustus.

"I was raised with Numaga," Augustus said, "Those men at the station kidnapped two innocent girls. Only a handful of us raided that station. There was no need for any retaliation against all the Paiutes. Ormsby and his cutthroats got exactly what they deserved."

"Do you remember trying to kill Cassidy?" Webster asked.

"I went after a coward that was running away from the fight, but I don't remember who he was. I thought I did kill him, too bad I failed."

"I think that's all the proof we need," Maxwell said. "Get hold of Judge Barnes and have him prepare for a trial in the morning."

The trial lasted less than an hour. Feelings were still strong about the men who were killed with Ormsby. Nothing anyone said in Augustus' defense made any difference. The scar on his chest was just as Cassidy described it.

The jury was back with its verdict in ten minutes. The courtroom was quiet as the judge read the verdict. "Kid, you've been found guilty by a jury of your peers. The charge is multiple murders, any one of which is a hanging offense. I sentence you to be hanged by the neck until you are dead. Execution will be day after tomorrow at noon. Court's adjourned." Martha was crying as Augustus was led away by four deputies.

The evening before the hanging, Webster allowed her to see Augustus. "I can't believe this is happening," she said holding his hands through the bars. Her eyes were red and she was worn-out. It was obvious she hadn't slept since the trial.

"Try not to take this too hard," Augustus said, "I told you I have obligations. It may be time to start fulfilling them."

"They're going to hang you."

"I know, but I believe it's my destiny. I'm not sorry for what we did to Ormsby. At least you're safe and they won't be trying to take your ranch anymore."

"But I love you," she said.

"I know. I wish I could have loved you."

"This can't be happening."

"You have to trust me," he said, "No matter what happens here tomorrow, it will be all right."

"Too bad this didn't turn out the way you wanted," Sam Cards said from an adjacent cell, "With the Kid out of the way, they'll have to turn us loose. It's Ms. Martha's word against ours. Nobody will believe her after this."

"Shut up, Cards," Webster said entering the room, "I'm sorry Ms. Hobbs, times up." Martha was sobbing as the marshal helped her up and escorted her out the door.

Jonas stepped in to help Martha and paused for a moment, "Son, I don't have the words."

"Jonas, you have to trust me," Augustus said, "This will all turn out all right. You just take care of Martha."

It was just before midnight when Burton Lee and Cassidy were walking back to the Nugget Hotel. They had been doing some drinking at a local saloon trying to figure a way to get back at the Hobbs' clan. They knew as soon as the Kid was dead, it would be a lot easier to do.

As they approached the hotel, a dark figure stepped out from between two buildings and blocked their path. "What do you want?" Cassidy asked.

Without saying a word, the dark figure came up with a rifle and fired. The quiet of the dark street was shattered as a bullet ripped through Burton Lee's heart, driving him to the ground and killing him instantly. Cassidy was in a panic and tried to draw his gun. Before he could get it out, the rifleman shot him in the hand. With his arm hanging limp by his side, Cassidy fell to his knees and began begging for his life.

"Why...ahhgg...did you do that?" he asked, gripping his mangled hand, "What do you want, I...I've got money, I'll. . . ."

He paused as the dark figure approached, worked the lever on the rifle, and stood over him. "It's you...no...please!" Without a word, the rifleman pressed the muzzle of the rifle to Cassidy's head and pulled the trigger. Blood and brain matter splattered on the sidewalk as the dark figure slipped away between the buildings. By the time anyone from the hotel got there, the only evidence left of the shooter was three empty .44 rim fire casings.

"Who is it?" Marshal Webster asked when he finally joined the crowd gathered around the bodies.

"It's Lee and Cassidy," one of his deputies said, checking the bodies, "Deader than hell, both of them."

"Did anybody see who did this?" Webster asked the people standing around him.

"It was one lone rifleman," a bystander said.

"What did he look like?"

"It was too dark to see," the man said, "He was lightly built, kind of gangly. He went through. . . ." Before the man could finish, two more shots rang out from down the street.

"What went on here," Webster demanded when he got to the jail.

"I...I don't know," the deputy replied, "I was out here when somebody killed Sam Cards and Carrot Top from the window of their cell."

"Did you see anybody?"

"It was dark and quiet when I got around back."

The day of the hanging was cloudy and threatening rain. Martha and Jonas were in attendance. Clay had left for Virginia City right after the trial. He had been drinking heavily and couldn't bear the thought of watching them hang Augustus.

The Governor was in front of the procession when they marched Augustus out of the jail and onto the gallows. Maxwell was finely dressed for his first official hanging. His black frock coat and striped gray pants were topped off with a stove-pipe hat. Martha was clinging to Jonas, trying not to pass out. Jonas was wiping the moisture from his eyes as he held her.

Augustus was quiet, remembering the words of Orpheus. If he was indeed invincible, he would soon know for sure. No matter how this went, he intended to endure it with dignity. His hands were tied behind as he stepped out onto the trapdoor. The hangman approached with the hood as the Governor turned to Augustus, "Any last words?" he asked.

"Go to hell," Augustus said. Jonas cracked a half-hearted smile.

A storm was approaching and the Governor wanted off the gallows before the rain ruined his fancy clothes. "Get on with it," he said, his right hand securing his top hat against the rising wind, "I'm late for lunch."

The wind grew stronger, making it difficult for the crowd to see through the swirling dust, as the hangman slipped the hood over Augustus' head. Martha was sobbing as the hangman placed the rope around Augustus' neck and tightened the noose. Stepping back, he took hold of the lever that would drop the trapdoor and waited for the signal. The Governor nodded and the trap was sprung.

Unable to bear it, Martha buried her face in her father's chest. A large dark shadow swept across the gallows just before the trapdoor fell and Augustus dropped through it. The startled crowd began to mumble among themselves as the marshal and the doctor calmly walked down the steps of the gallows to verify that Augustus was dead.

"Is it over?" Martha asked.

"I think so," Jonas said, "but something's not right. What was that thing?"

"I didn't see," Martha said, "What thing?"

"I don't rightly know. It was like a cloud of smoke or something surrounded Augustus just before they sprung the trapdoor."

Marshal Webster stuck his head out from under the gallows and looked up at the group of men still standing on the platform. Strangely concerned, he quickly disappeared back under the gallows. "Who the hell is that?" he demanded, seeing the stove-pipe hat lying on the ground and the striped gray pants on the body that several men were lowering to the ground.

Finding his hands suddenly free, Augustus yanked off his hood and discovered he was astride his big black horse. A strange, but somehow familiar man was riding alongside him. The day had suddenly turned to night as they headed west into a raging thunderstorm, "Am I ... dead?" Augustus asked.

"No," the man said, "Do you not remember my promise to you?"

"Promise...what promise?"

"We met many years ago, little brother, in the village along the lake."

"Perseus," Augustus declared, suddenly recognizing his companion, "Are you...are we actually together? It's been so long."

"Yes, together, just as I said."

101

"Over the years, I doubted you were real. I figured it was all a dream brought on after seeing those Indians killed."

"Is the scar on your chest real, and what of your horse?"

"Yeah," Augustus said, "I always thought you had something to do with this horse. He never seems to get any older."

"You will come to understand that he is much more than a mere horse. I promised to come for you when you were needed. You have done well and lived an honorable life. A great evil has come to the land of your grandfathers. It is time for you to join us."

"You couldn't have picked a better time," Augustus said, "They were about to hang me."

"That time is no more," Perseus said, "and we have much work to do."

"Where are we going?"

"A land that is nearby, but very far away. There is much trouble there. We will begin the battle from there. You, little brother will begin the fight alone," Perseus said, "Then the four of us will finish it."

"The four of us," Augustus said.

"Perseus, Theseus, Orpheus, and Augustus, Riders of the Dires, Sons of Chimalpopoca, together at last."

"Where are Theseus and Orpheus?"

"They will join us when we need them."

The rising sun found Augustus and Perseus still in the saddle. After riding through the night, they found themselves in an area of arid sagebrush flats nestled between steep rolling hills.

"Where the devil are we?" Augustus asked. Before Perseus could answer, a roaring crescendo of noise engulfed them. Augustus was in shock as a huge silver beast came over the hills to the north and soared right over his head. He very nearly fell out of the saddle trying to get a better look. "What...what the hell was that?"

Perseus sat quietly and chuckled at Augustus' reaction. They were just north of the outer markers for the Reno, Nevada Airport. "It is called an airplane," Perseus said.

"What kind of critter is an airplane?"

"It is not an animal. It is a flying machine that carries people all around the world. It can fly over the highest mountains and cross the country in a few hours."

"You mean to tell me there were people in that thing?"

"Yes, a hundred or more."

"A hundred," Augustus repeated, "that's unbelievable…all right, I know you've been around for a long time, but just exactly where are we?"

"We have been sent to do battle with evil once again," Perseus said, "in the 21st century."

"The 21st century, I can't believe…just what year is this?"

"It is 2010."

"Twenty…you mean, we just rode through a hundred and…a hundred-and-forty years last night?"

"Time and space are not barriers astride the Dires," Perseus said, "You are going to a place called The Reno Kid Ranch, but first we are going into the hills around the lake where this journey started. There is much you must learn before we can begin this fight."

Chapter Nine: The Silver State Stampede

It was going to be another hot day in Washington D.C. A graying man about sixty was sitting behind a huge oak desk in the Dirksen Senate Office Building. Still hung over from the fundraiser the night before, he was dozing when the intercom on the desk came alive. "Senator, there's a call for you from Reno, a Mr. Cassidy."

"Put him through," the senator said. "What's going on, Will?" he asked after picking up the phone.

"Have you seen the paper from out here this morning?" the voice on the other end asked.

"Can't say that I have, why do you ask?"

"There's another editorial from Teddy Hobbs."

"What now?"

"It's about a subsidiary of Far East and all the ecological damage they've done in China. He claims they dump more than seven million tons of toxic waste in a lake over there every year. Claims it's a byproduct from the manufacture of the neodymium batteries in the turbines. The damn lake has grown to be six miles wide over the last few years and the radiation levels are ten times above normal. The article goes on to say the farmers who live around there are developing lung and skin diseases. Their teeth are falling out and cancer rates have soared. Hobbs' claims any company with such a poor environmental record in their home country, shouldn't be supported by American tax dollars or allowed to do business in Nevada."

"We don't need that kind of publicity."

"What can I do about it? He can write whatever he wants. It's still a free country."

"Yes, but it should be the truth."

"From what I can find out it is the truth. Anybody with internet access can look it up for themselves."

"Schedule a meeting for next week. I'm coming out for the Stampede. Afterwards, we'll all get together in Carson City. If this project is ever going to fly, we have to find a way to shut Hobbs up."

"I'll do it, see you then."

"Welcome to the final day of the Silver State Stampede!" the announcer's voice proclaimed. It was a hot day in early July and the weather was dry. Eighty-five-year-old, Gordon Hobbs had just taken a seat in the stands nearest the bucking chutes.

Gordon Hobbs was a semi-retired stock contractor, who specialized in bucking bulls. In addition he was the patriarch of the Reno Kid Ranch, a sprawling cattle ranch in the Palomino Valley, just north of Reno, Nevada. Gordon was the great-grandson of Jonas Hobbs, founder of the ranch.

Gordon was an old school cowboy and rancher. He stood just over six-feet. He had a lean build, but aging with a little bit of a paunch. His hair was gray, but he could still saddle his own horse and he did a day's work every day. His word was law on the Reno Kid Ranch. Gordon had no use for slackers, celebrities, government workers, or politicians.

The old man got to his feet and removed his hat when a big American flag went by. He was paying close attention to the pretty little cowgirl that was carrying it. She was wearing a bright red, rhinestone studded outfit, a white John B. Stetson, and riding a spirited pinto mare. The cowgirl's long blonde curls were flying in the wind as she led the grand procession to open the day's events. "My great-granddaughter," Gordon said to the stranger in front of him.

"Mighty pretty," the stranger replied over his shoulder.

The bright red cowgirl circled the arena twice and rode to the center. Reining her horse to a stop, the pinto stood firm as the other riders formed a big circle around her and the flag. When they were all in place, a rousing rendition of the Star Spangled Banner blasted from the p.a. system.

After the anthem was over, the procession headed out of the arena and the crowd took their seats. "That was seventeen-year-old Ms. Haley Jackson," the announcer said, "Queen of your 2010 Silver State Stampede Cowgirl Court."

"Folks we have a special guest with us today," the announcer went on to say as the applause died down, "The Honorable Reed Henry, United States Senator from our great state of Nevada!" A heavy-set graying man about sixty stood up and waved his hat at the crowd. The applause was less than spectacular as the senator took his seat.

"Where have you been?" Gordon asked the young man who had just joined him in the stands.

"After the Ring of Fear last night, me and a couple of the boys went into town."

"And you got drunk," Gordon said, "Probably spent all your money doing it."

"No," the youngster said, "I lost all my money in a poker game a little later."

"Oh well then," Gordon said in disgust, "I feel better about the whole thing knowing that."

The young man with Gordon was his twenty-five-year-old grandson, Coltin Hobbs. He was better known as Colt by the rodeo cowboys and his many girlfriends. Colt was tall, tan, lean and Hollywood good looking. He was the youngest of Gordon's grandchildren, fun-loving, carefree, and basically worthless.

Colt dreamed of being a world famous bull rider, but so far that hadn't worked out and his other options were pretty limited. Unlike his older sister, Colt didn't pursue any higher education after high school. He figured being an heir to the Reno Kid Ranch, he had a job for life, and his looks would get him just about anything else he wanted.

"Didn't she look great," An attractive redhead asked as she took a seat next to Colt.

"Just like her mom," Colt said.

"Thank you, little brother," the redhead said, "How are you doing, Grandpa?"

"Never better," Gordon replied, "Haley's about the prettiest thing out there today."

"Yes she is," the redhead agreed. The redhead sitting with Colt and Gordon was thirty-four-year-old Charley Hobbs. She was Gordon's granddaughter and Colt's older sister. Charley had been married to a flashy and often unfaithful rodeo cowboy, but after a bitter divorce, she took back her maiden name. The only good thing to come out of the tumultuous marriage was Haley Jackson, Charley's daughter.

Charley Hobbs was tall for a woman and slender in build. Being a large animal veterinarian, Charley was strong-willed, stubborn, and rough-as-a-cob. She took care of all the stock at the Reno Kid Ranch and she maintained a clinic there for her other customers. Strong, confident, and financially independent, Charley was absolutely positive she would never remarry.

The three of them sat and watched as the last day go-rounds proceeded. When it was time for the bull riding, Colt excused himself and went to get ready. "What bull did Colt draw today?" Charley asked.

"Widow Maker," Gordon replied without looking around.

"That's not good," Charley said, "Who's on Shock Waves?"

"Some guy out of South Dakota," Gordon said, "Billy somebody, I never heard of him."

The old man was fidgety as he watched the chutes. If all went well, this ride could mean an invitation to the Finals in Las Vegas for Shock Waves. Gordon had been raising bucking bulls since 1956. He had some success over the years but only one National Champion. With all the TV exposure for bull riding, raising bucking bulls was becoming a big business and there was lots of competition. Shock Waves was from the blood-lines of War Bonnet, undoubtedly the most famous champion bull ever raised on the Reno Kid Ranch.

With the cattle markets down and taxes at an all time high, The Reno Kid Ranch was in bad need of another champion bull. Over the years, many of War Bonnet's progeny had done well on the circuit, but Gordon was hoping Shock Waves would put him back at the forefront.

"There he is," Gordon said when he finally spotted Shock Waves being loaded in the chute. When the bull was secure, a short stocky young cowboy climbed up on the chute and began to descend onto Shock Waves. The cautious cowboy was wearing a Kevlar vest, a helmet, and a full face mask. "You better get a good hold, South Dakota" Gordon said with grin, "You're damn sure gonna need it."

When the cowboy was finally aboard, he gave the gateman a nod and the battle was on. Old Shock Waves blasted out of the chute, faked to the right and immediately spun to the left. His hind legs were so high in the air it looked like he was standing on his head, but the South

Dakota cowboy was hanging right with him as the battle raged. Shock Waves went into a left-handed spin as the time clicked down. When he had the cowboy fully committed to the spin, the wily bull switched direction.

After hitting the dirt of the arena, South Dakota just managed to get to his feet and grab the top rail before old Shock Waves hooked the seat of the fallen cowboy's pants and boosted him over into the alley.

"Sorry, Billy," the announcer said, "That was one heck of a ride but about a half-second too short. How 'bout that Shock Waves?" he said to the crowd, "he is something else. Ya'll give that cowboy a big hand for staying with that rank bull for as long as he did."

"That ride didn't hurt us none," Charley said.

"Yep," Gordon replied, "That ornery bull did real good."

"Here comes, Colt," Charley said. "I hope he don't get killed, he owes me a hundred bucks."

Gordon laughed at her twisted sense of humor. "I hope not too," he said. "But look at him, no helmet, no faceguard."

"He's too pretty to cover all that up," Charley said with a little sarcasm, "he wants to look good for the ladies who'll be down at the Horse Shoe Club tonight."

"He's too damn tall to be a bull rider," Gordon said, "He won't look too good to anybody, if he gets his face smashed in or his fool neck broke."

"Next man out of the chute is Nevada cowboy Colt Hobbs from down in Reno," the announcer said, "Colt's drawn Widow Maker. For all you unattached ladies out there, Colt is a single cowboy, so regardless of what happens in the next eight seconds, there won't be any widows made here today."

Colt got himself in position, pulled his hat down to his eyebrows and gave a nod. When the gate swung open, Widow Maker gave a half-hearted leap into the arena. That split-second of non-performance gave Colt a dangerous shot of over-confidence. Before Colt could figure out what went wrong, Widow Maker came up with his shoulders, went high to the right with his hind legs and launched Colt into the air. The last thing Colt would remember about this ride was Widow Maker's big head coming right at his face.

Colt was out cold and laying face-down in the dirt when the bullfighters yanked him up and started dragging him toward the fence. "He'll be alright, folks," the announcer said. "They tell me he just had the wind knocked out of him. Give that cowboy a big Elko hand. That was the most exciting one-point-seven seconds of the afternoon!"

Early next morning, Gordon was loading Shock Waves into his trailer. "Morning Gramps," Haley said when she walked up.

"Morning," Gordon said, "You all about ready to go?"

"Mom's loaded and ready," she said, "We're just waiting on Uncle Colt."

"You all go ahead, I'll get Colt. He can ride back with me."

"Okay then," she said giving Gordon a kiss on the cheek, "See you at home."

It was close to sundown when Charley and Haley turned off the highway at Left Hand Canyon and went through the gates of The Reno Kid Ranch. It only took a moment to unload the pinto and unhook the trailer. Looking back down the access road, there was no sign of Gordon and Colt.

When they entered the back door to the house, Haley saw a man sitting at the kitchen table. "Hi, Pa," Haley said, "We're home, in case you haven't noticed."

"You two are hard to miss," he said, "How did it go?"

"You would have been proud, Dad," Charley said, "Haley was elected the Queen."

"I already heard," he said, "It was all over the news last night. Wish I could have been there."

The man at the table was sixty-two-year-old Theodore Roosevelt Hobbs, better known to most as Teddy. He was Gordon's son and Charley's father. Teddy retired early from his aeronautical engineering job in Portland, and came home to the ranch. He kept his commercial pilot's license current as he did quite a bit of traveling.

Teddy started a small independent consulting firm involved with the mounting environmental issues facing the ranchers, and the war being waged against them by the well-funded and politically powerful Green Energy movement.

As they were talking, they heard Gordon's diesel pull up outside. It was only a minute before Colt came through the door with a taped-up broken nose and two very prominent black eyes. "What in blazes happened to you?" Teddy asked.

"Widow Maker," Colt mumbled, "That's what happened to me."

"Smile for him," Charley said.

"No," Colt said, "leave me alone."

"C'mon, Uncle Colt," Haley said, "Just a little one."

Colt couldn't hold it in any longer and he had to grin. His lips parted, revealing two missing front teeth on the top. "It's no worse than the other times," he said, "I'll go into Reno tomorrow and get 'em fixed."

"Maybe you ought to think about another line of work," Teddy said.

"Or investing in a catcher's mask," Charley added.

"Very funny, Sis, that's very funny," Colt replied. Leaving his family alone, the battered and bruised bull rider limped out the door and headed toward the bunkhouse. Colt lived in the bunkhouse with their hired hand. It made him feel more like a cowboy instead of the privileged grandson of the owner. It also afforded him the freedom to come and go as he pleased, regardless of the hour and without being interrogated by his family.

"I see you made it back," Gordon said to Teddy when he entered the house.

"I got in about an hour ago."

"How did it go?"

"It's not good, Dad," Teddy said. "I don't know who's behind all of this, but these Green Power people have support in high political places. I'm afraid those wind turbines are going to be all around us if we aren't careful."

"The damn things are eyesores," Gordon said. "Some of those flannel mouthed sons-o. . . ." He paused after seeing Haley paying close attention. "Some of those people talked Ed Taylor into putting one up on his place. Ed claims it makes so much noise he can't sleep nights. He can't watch TV for the interference and he's found three dead eagles under it in less than six months."

"But Gramps," Haley said, "We need to find ways to make clean energy so we can get away from using so much foreign oil."

"That's true," Teddy said, "But these windmills are more about money than clean energy. The government is offering huge sums of grant money to anybody who is willing to develop that technology. It's a political thing, trying to make the current administration look like they're actually doing something. It matters little to any of them in Washington whether it works or not, just how it looks."

"I hear they're already going up on the federal land east of here," Charley said.

"You can thank Reed Henry for that," Teddy said, "He's in this up to his eyeballs. I just haven't found a way to prove it yet."

"You need to be careful, Daddy," Charley said. "These people could be dangerous."

"Dangerous," Gordon repeated, "I wish I had old Jonas Hobbs, Grandpa Clay, and the Reno Kid here now, I'd show them green sons-o-bitches dangerous."

The conversation ended on that note and everyone retired to their rooms to get ready for supper. After Colt got himself cleaned up, he rejoined them in the main house. After a nice family meal, Charley was clearing the table when Haley asked a question, "Gramps, who was Grandpa Clay and the Reno Kid?"

"Clay was Jonas Hobbs' son, and my grandfather. Jonas was the founder of this ranch, back in the 1850's he called it the Lost Jackass Ranch."

"That's a funny name," Haley said.

"There was some story behind it, but I don't recall what it was," Gordon said, "Clay was kind of an easy going fellow; a lot like you're Uncle Colt." Colt cracked another toothless smile as Gordon continued, "After meeting the man they came to know as the Reno Kid, Clay changed. He became a responsible rancher, married later in life and had my dad."

"What about the Reno Kid?" Haley asked.

"He had a name, but I don't know if I ever heard it," Gordon said.

"It was Augustus," Charley said.

"How would you know that?" Teddy asked.

"You remember, Dad" Charley said, "When we were tearing down the original old house, we found Great Aunt Martha's trunk."

"I suppose I remember that," Teddy said.

"When I was going through it, I found Aunt Martha's diary. She was obviously in love with the Reno Kid. So much so she never got over him. Martha never married. She died an old lady, right here on the ranch."

"What happened to the Reno Kid?" Haley asked.

"That's where the story gets really strange," Charley said.

"The Kid was a brutal gunfighter," Gordon said, "The railroad was trying to take this ranch when he showed up. The stories my grandfather used to tell about him were almost more than I could believe. Grandpa Clay was so grateful to the Kid; he renamed the ranch after him when Jonas died."

"So, the railroad never got the ranch," Haley said.

"The Kid saw to that," Gordon said, "but the crooked politicians eventually hung him for it."

"Hung him!" Haley said.

"Maybe not," Charley said, "Some of the entries in Martha's diary were made just before his hanging. She was heartbroken. But right after the hanging she seemed to believe he was still alive. I think she spent the rest of her life waiting for him to return."

"Were Martha and the Kid lovers?" Colt asked.

"Indeed they were," Charley said, "She described him pretty well, if you know what I mean."

"I think I do," Colt said, "But I don't want to hear about it."

"I do," Haley said.

"Maybe later," Charley said, "Right now you need to help me with these dishes and get ready for school tomorrow."

"But I'm the queen," Haley protested.

"That was in Elko," Charley said, "But you're not. . . ."

"No, she's right," Colt said, getting up from the table. "You just relax, Your Majesty. I'll help your mother with the dishes, but just this once."

The next morning a meeting was being held behind closed doors in Senator Reed Henry's, Carson City office. There were representatives from the local power company, an international investment company from Mexico City, a wind turbine manufacturer from China, and the Nevada alternative energy committee chairman.

"We are way behind," Senator Henry warned the group. "We have the funding from the Federal grants and we have the federal loan guarantees for the money we're borrowing from Juan's bank. The state tax credits have been approved. What is the problem?"

"There are eight complete 2.5 megawatt turbines sitting on the dock in San Diego as we speak," Don Chow said, "And eight more waiting to be loaded in Haikow. The problem is not with us." Don Chow was the U.S. representative from the Far East Wind Energy Corporation, a China based wind turbine manufacturer.

"Well it damn sure isn't with my bank," Juan Carlos said, "we've already paid Far East twenty-eight million dollars for the turbines in San Diego and the funding is in place for the one's sitting in China."

"That just leaves you, Cassidy," Senator Henry said.

"This kind of thing takes time," Will Cassidy explained. "None of these ranchers want those damn turbine towers on their land. The plans to put them up on BLM land is stalled in committee in Washington. The tree-huggers are having a field day." Cassidy was the chairman of the Nevada Alternative Energy Committee.

"I'm flying back to Washington tonight," Henry said, "I'll get the White House to give that committee a swift kick in the ass. The President wants this project well underway before the next election and we have to account for at least part of this money."

"What about the ranchers?" Juan asked.

"The worst is old man Hobbs and his family out at the Reno Kid Ranch," Cassidy said, "His son, Teddy, is the one stirring up most of the tree-huggers. He has made it his personal crusade to keep the turbines off the mountains around the Palomino Valley."

"I think maybe we need some outside help with this Old Man Hobbs and his son," Chow said, "I have associates that deal with this kind of resistance."

"Let me talk to him one more time," Cassidy said, "If I don't get anywhere with him, then we'll take this to the next level."

"Be damn quick about it," Henry warned, "Time is running out. We have to start building to keep those grants. If this deal falls through, there will be too many questions asked about where the money went."

"That is true," Carlos said, "My stockholders will demand. . . ."

"We all know who your stockholders are," Henry said, "They may run your country, but I can make it extremely difficult for them here. They would do well to stay out of this."

"If they think some of their money has been, how should I say this, misappropriated, it will be very bad for everyone involved."

"Please," Chow said, "Everyone just keep your head. There is too much at stake for our coalition to fall apart now."

"He's right," Henry agreed, "We'll take care of the Hobbs' and then we'll start building. Chow, get your people headed this way, if Cassidy fails, we'll do it your way."

That evening, Gordon and the family were sitting on the porch of the main house, enjoying a little peace and quiet at the end of their day. Gordon sat up and looked down the access road when he spotted a car approaching. "Who do you suppose that is?" he asked.

"Don't know the car," Teddy said, "Maybe it's someone for Charley."

"I'm not expecting anyone," she said.

The car pulled up in front of the house and an average sized man got out. He was dressed in a suit, but no tie. "Good evening, everyone," he said when he got to the porch.

"Good evening," Teddy said, "Can we help you?"

"I hope so," the man said, "I'm Will Cassidy from the Alternative Energy Committee. We need to talk."

"Cassidy," Charley repeated, "That name rings a bell, but I don't. . . ."

"Probably thinking about my great-grandfather," Cassidy said, "He practically settled this whole area single handed."

"You don't say," Gordon said.

"Yes sir," Cassidy said, "At first his family thought he'd been killed by Indians, but years later they found out he was at William's Station the night of the Paiute raid. After he ran the Indians off, he rode all night to Virginia City and raised a militia. He came back with Ormsby."

"Did he die with Ormsby and the rest?" Gordon asked.

"No, but he lost an eye. In spite of being gravely wounded, he continued to fight. The men with him claimed they never saw anything like it. My family claims they wanted to name the city after him. Cassidyville, I think they said. Grandpa wouldn't hear of it. He said Major Reno was a hero and he deserved the honor. My great-grandpa was a modest man."

"What finally happened to this legendary great-grandpa of yours?" Colt asked.

"The Reno Kid's gang ambushed him in Carson City. They say he got five or six of them before one of them got in a lucky shot. Biggest funeral ever held in Nevada, they say."

"Mighty interesting story," Gordon said, "Now what brings you out here, Mr. Cassidy?"

"Mr. Hobbs, we have a national crisis on our hands."

"Is that so?"

"Yes, we need a source of renewable energy that doesn't contribute to global warming."

"A lot of people don't believe there is such a thing as global warming," Teddy said, "I happen to be one of them."

"Mr. Hobbs," Cassidy said to Gordon, "The state of Nevada is committed to leading the way with the new wind generated power technology. We would very much like to put several turbines on those hills above your house."

"That will never happen," Gordon said.

"They will be up on those ridges to your east," Cassidy said, "That's BLM land and we will get the permits, eventually."

"That would require a public referendum," Teddy said.

"We've already held several public meetings about that."

"That's true," Teddy said, "Only you forgot to invite the public. The first any of us heard about that meeting was in the paper the day after it was over."

"I'm sure that was an oversight on someone's part."

"Let me make this easy for you, Mr. Cassidy," Gordon said, "I'm the only one here who has ever been in combat."

"Combat," Cassidy said, "Nobody's talking about. . . ."

"Italy, 1943," Gordon said. "I'm pretty sure I'm the only one here who has ever killed a man."

"I'm sure that's true," Cassidy said, "But, I don't see where. . . ."

"If you or any of your people try to put one of those turbines on my ranch, I'll kill every damn one of you, and coming from me, Mr. Cassidy, that's no idle threat."

"I'm sure you don't mean that...if we could just. . . ."

"Get off my ranch, Mr. Cassidy," Gordon warned, "And don't come back."

"What do you think about that?" Charley asked when Cassidy was gone.

"I think we got big problems," Teddy said, getting to his feet.

"Where are you going?" Gordon asked.

"To call Clark Brown down at Silver State Leasing before they close, see if I can get the King Air."

"Why do you need the plane?" Charley asked.

"There's an EPA meeting in Sacramento on Wednesday, I plan to be there."

"Isn't the King Air more plane than you really need just to fly to Sacramento?" Gordon asked. "Money doesn't grow on trees around here, you know."

"Believe me, Dad, I know, but I like to have a little more power under me when I cross the Sierras. You never know what the weather and the winds are going to be like up there."

The following Wednesday, the Sacramento environmental impact meeting lasted for hours. A string of government experts went on and on about the advantages of wind turbine produced power. They showed slick, Hollywood produced, videos featuring B-list celebrities and retired politicians, all singing the praises of wind energy.

It was mid-afternoon before Teddy got an opportunity to address the panel and ask a few questions. "Mr. Chairman," he said, "Isn't it true that property values plummet when the towers are placed in a community?"

"There is some speculation about that," the chairman said, "but no studies have been made to prove it."

"That's not exactly accurate," Teddy said, shuffling the papers in front of him, "I have a report here about a man in Michigan who lives over two thousand feet from a turbine and he has to play music all day to drown out the humming. Not only that, but every morning between eight and nine, his house is invaded by pulsing shadows as the blades turn in the rising sunlight. Those shadow pulses are common wherever these turbines have been installed. Those same shadow pulses have been reported to cause seizures in some people."

"The government has no knowledge of that."

"The low frequency sound pressure is repetitive. It never stops. Some of his neighbors have been forced to move to escape the onslaught, and have lost their homes to foreclosure, because they can't find anyone crazy enough to buy them."

"Again," the chairman said, "There are no government funded studies to prove that. I'm afraid it's just hearsay."

"Very well," Teddy said, "U.S. Fish and Wildlife, an agency of the federal government, I believe, estimates nearly half-a-million birds are killed annually by these spinning turbines. Most of them endangered raptors, eagles, hawks, buzzards, and so forth."

"That may be true, but we can't hold up this program on account of a few birds."

"Is that so," Teddy said. "It's a matter of record that your agency cancelled the construction of a multi-million-dollar hydro-electric dam in Tennessee because of a tiny fish that most people had never heard of.

And don't even get me started on what the spotted owls have cost the lumber industry in the northwest."

"If there is a point to all of this," the chairman said, "Please get to it."

"I have just one more question," Teddy said.

"Thank goodness, what is it."

"Is it not true, that the bearings in these turbines have to be heated in the winter to prevent them from freezing up and snapping the blades off? In fact, it's already happened in North Dakota. The truth is, they don't generate enough electricity to heat themselves and the power has to come from the commercial grid?"

"We are working on that problem," the chairman said, "and your time is up, please make your point and sit down."

"The people of Great Britain have spent billions on wind farms. Their total turbine generated power amounts to less than two-percent of the total annual electric output, and cost twice as much as conventionally produced electricity."

"This is your last warning, Mr. Hobbs, make your point," the chairman said, "It's late."

"The point is this," Teddy said, "Wind energy is based on bad science. As it currently stands, it's more about greed energy than green energy."

"Who the hell is he?" the chairman asked the man next to him as Teddy took his seat.

"Teddy Hobbs," the man said, "from Reno."

"He's a pain in the ass. When this fiasco is over, get Reed Henry on the phone."

"Are you coming home tonight?" Charley asked when Teddy called from Sacramento to tell her about the meeting.

"No," he said, "It's already dark, it's raining in the mountains, and I'm beat. I'll be home tomorrow."

"Have a good night," Charley said, "I love you."

"I love you too," he said, "Good night."

It was a little after nine when Will Cassidy's cell phone rang. "Cassidy," the voice on the other end said.

"Yes sir, what is it."

"We got to do something about Teddy Hobbs. He's going to spoil this whole deal."

"The old man too," Cassidy said, "He threatened to kill me the last time I was out there."

"You may be right, they both need to go. Write down this number. It's a guy I know in San Francisco. Pay attention, here's what I want you to tell him."

The next afternoon, Charley was finishing up when Gordon walked into her clinic. "We should have heard from Teddy by now," he said, "Do you think something could have happened?"

"He's probably been delayed by the weather," she said.

"The weather has cleared all the way to California, I checked."

"Let's go in and call the airport in Reno, maybe he filed an amended flight plan."

Colt and Haley were listening along with Gordon as Charley spoke to the tower in Reno, "No...I don't know for sure...I'll hold." She placed her hand over the phone as she waited. "They are going to call Sacramento," she said, "to see what time he left, if he has."

Removing her hand from the phone the other's watched as Charley's face turned pale. "He did...and no one has heard from him since then? What can we do? You will? Yes, yes, we'll be right here, thank you."

"What is it?" Gordon asked as she hung up the phone.

"Dad left before noon. There has been no contact with his plane. He should have been here hours ago."

"What are they doing?" Colt asked.

"The tower is notifying the authorities and they will hopefully get organized and start searching."

"Come on," Colt said, "We need to go!"

"Go where?" Gordon asked. "The best thing we can do is stay here. Your dad is a good pilot. If he had trouble, he probably made it down okay…somewhere. We'll hear from him."

It was nearly midnight when they were startled by the ringing phone. "Yes…yes, this is Ms. Hobbs," Charley said into the phone. "I'm putting you on the speaker so the others can hear."

"Ms. Hobbs," the voice on the other end said, "We have sent bulletins to every law enforcement, military, and rescue agency in both states. No one has heard anything of your father. The search is set to get underway as soon as there's enough light. I'm afraid that's all we can do tonight."

"I understand," Charley said, "Please let me know if you hear anything…anything at all."

"I'll do that, Ms. Hobbs," the voice assured her, "Good night."

"I can't believe this is happening," Charley said, hanging up the phone, "What if?"

"We'll deal with that if we have to," Gordon said, "for now, we can't give up hope. I'm going down to Reno, you two stay here by the phone."

"There really isn't anything you can do down there," Charley said.

"I know, but I just feel like some of us should be there."

It took close to an hour for Gordon to make the drive down to the Reno airport. He found an empty spot and parked his old Jeep Wrangler. It was getting more and more difficult for the old man to get in and out of the cramped Jeep, but he loved driving it. The lights were still on at Silver State Aircraft Leasing. "Mr. Hobbs," the man behind the desk said as Gordon entered, "I wasn't expecting you down here tonight."

"You're here kind o' late, Clark," Gordon said. Clark Brown owned the leasing company and the plane Teddy was flying.

"Teddy's a friend of mine," Clark said, "I just felt like I should be here…in case…you know."

"What do you think happened?"

"I don't know, but it's unlikely it was trouble with the airplane."

"Airplanes come down all the time," Gordon said.

"I know accidents happen, but that plane is among the safest there is. It's equipped with two Merlin engines, even if one failed completely, which isn't likely. Teddy could have made it back on the other one. How was Teddy's health? Is it possible he could have had a heart attack or something?"

"Not likely," Gordon said, "He's pretty healthy."

"There's fresh coffee over there," Clark said, "help yourself." "As soon as it's light, I'm taking off."

"Where are you going?"

"I'm going to back-track Teddy's flight plan to Sacramento. I can't just sit here and do nothing. There's a locator beacon in the plane that should have been activated if he was forced down. I'm going to try and pick it up."

"Can I go with you?" Gordon asked.

"I think it would be best if you didn't," Clark said, "I'm taking my old Piper. I want to go low and slow. There isn't much room and it could be pretty bumpy."

"I suppose you're right," Gordon said, "I never was fond of flying. I don't know where Teddy gets it. . . ." Gordon was interrupted by the ringing telephone."

"Hello," Clark said, "Yes sir, how are you? No, there's been no word. I'll be taking off as soon as it's light. Mr. Hobbs is here now. That's right, Gordon Hobbs. Yes sir, I'll tell him."

"Who was that?" Gordon asked.

"Senator Henry," Clark said. "I suppose word of Teddy's disappearance has made the news in Washington. He said to assure you that everything that can be done will be."

As soon as the eastern sky began to lighten, Clark got ready to go. "Mr. Hobbs," he said, "I need to lock up. You need to go home and get some sleep. I'll call you if I see or hear anything at all."

"I appreciate that," Gordon said, "And you be careful up there."

Having been up all night, Gordon was having trouble keeping his eyes open on the ride home. He was north of Spanish Springs, just passed the spot where the road narrows down to two lanes, when he noticed a fast approaching vehicle in his rear view mirror. It seemed to be a pickup or a large sport utility.

"That damn fool is gonna kill somebody," Gordon said to himself as the vehicle grew large in his mirror. At the last moment, the speeding vehicle slowed, but instead of veering around Gordon, it rammed the Jeep from behind. Gordon was fighting the wheel as the Wrangler shot forward and left the road. The old man couldn't hold it as the careening Jeep rocketed through the sagebrush, hit a gulley, and rolled over three times.

Charley had been awake off and on all through the night. She just dozed off again when the phone rang. Colt spent the night in the main house to be near Charley and Haley in case bad news came. The phone call woke him up. He was hopping down the hall trying to get one leg in his jeans and straining to hear what Charley was saying.

"What is it?" he asked when she hung up.

"Its Grandpa," she said, "He's been in an accident. Get dressed, we have to go."

"What happened?" Haley asked from the back seat as they sped toward Reno.

"The officer that called said there were no other vehicles involved and no one saw it happen. He thinks Grandpa fell asleep driving home this morning."

"Did he say how Gramps was?" Haley asked.

"The officer didn't know, but they did life-flight him. Considering his age, this may not be good."

"We're here for Gordon Hobbs," Charley said to the receptionist at the front desk of the hospital.

"Hobbs," the lady repeated as she searched her computer screen, "Mr. Hobbs is in the trauma center. Take this hallway, third door on the right. Someone will meet you in the waiting area."

Charley paced back and forth while they waited. It seemed like forever before a nurse came by and told them Gordon was still alive, but undergoing emergency surgery. She promised to update them as soon as there was any word.

Finally after three hours, the doctor appeared. "Are you folks here for Gordon Hobbs?" he asked.

"Yes," Charley said, suddenly on her feet, "How is he?"

"He's a tough old bird," the doctor said. Charley relaxed just a little after hearing that and seeing the smile on the doctor's face. "There was some internal damage. He lost his spleen and a lot of blood, but I think he'll recover. He has a bad neck sprain and his right leg is broken in two places. An orthopedist will have to put a pin in it, in a few days, when he's stronger."

"Can we see him?"

"As soon as he's out of recovery, but I'll warn you now, he's bruised all over and he looks much worse than he is. He probably won't be making much sense when you speak to him. We'll be keeping him pretty well drugged up until his next surgery. That leg is going to hurt for a while."

"Thanks Doc," Colt said.

"Yes," Charley said, "Thank you so much."

It was a week later when Charley and Haley were walking down the corridor to Gordon's room. They could hear the old man reading the riot act to somebody. "I'm a veteran," Gordon said to the nurse, "I've been in combat, the big one, World War Two. I've seen men hurt worse than this and keep right on fighting. The Tenth Mountain Division didn't run the damn Nazis out of Italy by sitting on our ass in a hospital every time we got a little ding."

"This was much more than a ding you old sidewinder," the nurse said, "and you ain't in the Tenth Mountain Division any more. I'd like nothing better than to get rid of your wrinkled old ass, but you ain't leaving here until the doctors say so."

"Is that a fact," Gordon said, "Well let me tell you one damn. . . ."

"Good morning, Ms. Hobbs," the nurse said, seeing Charley walk in the room, "He's doing well this morning."

"So I hear," Charley said.

"I'll leave you alone to visit with your family," the nurse said to Gordon, "but I'll be back."

"Thanks for the warning," Gordon said to her back.

"Does she always speak to you like that?" Charley asked after the nurse was gone.

"Yep," Gordon said, "I like her. She's the only one here that'll give me a straight answer. The rest of them just tuck their tail and run."

"The doctor says you can go home Friday," Haley said with her arm around his shoulders. "I'm gonna be your nurse after that."

"Colt's going to bring the dually down so you can stretch out in the back seat." Charley said.

"How's he doing with me and Teddy gone?"

"You wouldn't know him," Charley said. "He's taken over. Between him and Glenn, things are running smooth."

"How's the Jeep?" Gordon asked.

"Colt towed it back to the ranch, but I'm afraid it's done for."

"If it was a horse," Haley said with a big grin, "We'd have to shoot it."

"That's not very funny. I'll miss that old Jeep."

"Gramps," Haley said, "Next time you go to town and stay up all night, you better let one of us go with you."

"Regardless of what the cops told you," Gordon said in a low voice, "I didn't fall asleep."

"What are you talking about?" Charley asked.

"A big black pickup, or something similar, followed me out of town that morning."

"Followed you," Charley repeated.

"They stayed way back until we got out on the two lane. Then they ran me off the road."

"We have to tell the police," Charley said.

"No," Gordon said, "With Teddy missing and me out of the way, they thought they could finally get what they want."

"They," Charley said, "Who's they?"

"Something bad is going on here, Charley, and I think I know who's behind it."

Chapter Ten: The Return of the Reno Kid

Two more weeks went by with no further word about Teddy. None of them would say so, but they were all pretty sure Teddy was gone. As long as they didn't know for certain, they would continue clinging to the hope he would be found alive. Life returned to normal, or about as normal as the family could possibly make it.

There was plenty of work to be done on the ranch and they had no choice but to get on with their lives. Gordon got home all right, but with at least three months left to go in a cast, he spent most of the time sitting on the front porch with his leg propped up.

Early one afternoon, Colt was sitting with the old man, when he spotted a dark suburban turn off the highway and come through the gate. "Who do you suppose that is?" Colt asked getting to his feet.

"I don't know," Gordon said, "Maybe they have word about Teddy."

When the suburban was parked, three heavyset men and one smaller one got out. All of them were well dressed and appeared to be Chinese. "Are you Gordon Hobbs?" the small man asked.

"That's me," Gordon said, "What do you men want?"

"I am Chai Ming," the small man said, "I have a paper for you to sign."

"A paper," Colt said, "What kind of paper?"

Before Ming could answer, Charley stepped out on the porch. "Good evening, Ms. Hobbs," Ming said.

"Good evening," she replied, "Do I know you?"

"I am Chai Ming, your humble servant, but my name is unimportant."

"What about this paper?" Gordon asked.

"It is a paper saying we can erect eight wind turbines on your property."

"You can take that paper and. . . ."

"I wouldn't be too hasty," Ming said. "You will be well paid."

"I already got all the money I need," Gordon said.

"Is this your daughter?" Ming asked, turning to Charley. He produced a photograph from his coat pocket. It was a picture of Haley standing in front of the high school.

"Yes, but. . . ."

"You have already lost a father. You almost lost a grandfather. It would be a shame to also lose a daughter."

"What do you know about my father? If you've done something to Haley. . . ."

"She is perfectly safe, we have done nothing to her," Ming said, "But if you want to keep her safe, you will. . . ."

Before Ming could finish he was drowned out by the sound of an approaching vehicle. They were all watching as a twenty-year-old F-150 regular cab pickup, with glass-packed mufflers and rusted out fenders, rolled into the yard. A one-horse bumper hitched trailer was hooked on the back as the old truck pulled up and stopped. The dust was still swirling as the driver started to get out without turning the key. When he took his foot off the clutch, the pickup bucked forward for a couple of feet until the engine died. A big black horse was stomping around, trying to maintain his balance in the lurching trailer.

"I can't get used to those contrary things," the stranger said with a grin. He was tall, dark, and lean with strong features. The stranger wore jeans and an un-tucked denim shirt with the sleeves rolled up to the elbows. Hatless, he ran his fingers through his long black hair, pushing it back out of his face as he walked toward the four Chinamen.

"What is it you want here?" Ming asked.

"Me," the stranger said, "Nothing, much."

"Why are you here?"

"Looking for a job. Why are you here?"

"That is for me to know," Ming said, "This is none of your concern, if you are smart, you will. . . ."

"Mr. Hobbs," the stranger said, turning to Gordon, "I hear you might be looking for some help."

"I might be at that," Gordon said.

"You must leave here at once or. . . ."

"I'm speaking to Mr. Hobbs," the stranger said to Ming.

"It is most unwise for you. . . ."

"It would be most unwise for you to push me much further," the stranger warned, turning to Ming.

In an attempt to silence the unwanted intruder, Ming motioned to one of his enforcers. The big man tried to grab the mouthy stranger but the stranger was too quick for him. As soon as the enforcer touched him, the stranger blocked the big man's hands and gave him a brutal knife-hand thrust to the throat. The suddenly helpless enforcer went to the ground gasping for air.

Before the others could join in, the stranger's feet left the ground and delivered a wicked spinning kick to the nearest man's head, dropping him. The third man lost his nerve and fled to the suburban for a weapon. Before he could reach it, the dark stranger landed a flying kick in the middle of his back, driving him face-first into the door of the suburban and knocking him out cold.

With the enforcers out of the way, the stranger reached under the back of his shirt, came up with a Berretta 92, and walked back to Ming. The once inscrutable little man was nervous as the stranger stood over him. Ming was staring down the barrel of the .40 as the stranger grabbed him by the collar and pressed the Berretta to the little man's forehead. "You made a big mistake when you threatened that little girl."

"No...I would not...how did you. . . ."

Before Ming could finish, the stranger cocked the hammer, "Take your friends and get out of this valley. Never come back here. If you return, I'll kill all of you. If you bring any harm to that little girl, I will hunt you down. Make no mistake about that. There is nowhere on this earth you can hide from me." Thumbing the safety, he replaced the Berretta in his belt and let Ming go.

"Who the hell are you?" Gordon asked after the Chinese were gone.

"I have to call the sheriff," Charley said as she turned to go inside.

"No," the stranger said, "Don't call anyone. No one will find those killers. They're hired assassins in this country illegally. They probably snuck in from Mexico and they'll leave the same way. Trust me it would be a waste of time."

"Trust you," Charley said, "You were ready to kill all four of those men."

"They were likely going to kill some of you if you wouldn't sign that paper," the stranger said, "If they return, I will kill them."

"What's your name?" Colt asked.

"My friends call me Reno," the stranger said.

"Reno," Gordon repeated, "Now there's a coincidence for you. Have you ever heard of the…no that's…no."

"Are you really here about a job?" Charley inquired.

"I would like to stay around until this trouble is over."

"Why are you so interested in our trouble?" Charley asked. The stranger standing there with them appeared to be in his forties, but extremely fit. With his long black hair, dark complexion, and chiseled features, the stranger was a handsome man. There was something in his sparkling dark eyes that seemed familiar to Charley. She wasn't sure what, but it was almost as if she knew him.

"It's just what I do, Ma'am," Reno replied. "It's sort of a calling, you might say."

"We're mighty glad you're here," Gordon said, "Toss your gear in the bunkhouse and put your horse out there in the corral, we'll have supper directly."

"Thank you," Reno said, "Sounds good. If you'll excuse me, ma'am," he said turning back to Charley.

"It's Charley," she said.

"I beg your pardon."

"It's Charley, not ma'am."

"Yes ma'am…Charley."

Reno got back in his pickup, started the engine and ground a couple of gears before finally heading it to the bunkhouse. "I hate these damn things!" he shouted to Gordon, "Give me a horse any day!"

"Amen to that," Gordon said with a big grin.

"Grandpa," Colt said, after Reno was gone.

"Yeah," Gordon replied.

"You remember wishing Grandpa Clay and the Reno Kid would come back to help us."

"I believe I do remember saying that, why?"

"From here on out, I'd be careful about what I wished for."

"I think you may be right, Colt, I surely do think you may be right."

"You can't be serious," Charley said, turning on her heel and heading in the house.

"I better go get him settled in," Colt said, leaving Gordon on the porch.

There's plenty of room," Colt said as he and Reno walked through the door of the bunkhouse, "It's just me and Rosebud out here now."

"Rosebud," Reno repeated.

"Glenn Rosebud," the other man in the room said, getting to his feet, "What of it?"

Glenn looked to be a typical rodeo cowboy with a big buckle on his belt and a chip on his shoulder. He was sturdily built, but not too tall. He looked to be in his thirties with a bushy mustache. Glenn wore a faded and battered old black cowboy hat and three days worth of whiskers on his chin.

"Just in case you got anything smart to say about my name," Glenn said walking up to Reno, "You can just save it, 'cause I've more 'n likely already heard it."

"What would I have to say about a cowboy named Glenn?" Reno asked with a grin. "I'm Reno. It's good to meet you."

"Glenn here is our ranch manager." Colt said, as Glenn shook Reno's hand. "He works with the bulls. He's in charge of making them overconfident."

"I don't understand," Reno said.

"Glenn is so easy to throw, the bulls get to thinking they're pretty good at it. I guess seeing him go flying through the air gives 'em a lot of confidence. Course that all changes when they come up on a real cowboy like me."

"A real cowboy," Glenn repeated and turned to Reno, "The last thing he ever stayed on for more than eight seconds was a loose woman down at the Ho Hum Motel. Even then, the manager had to throw him out for yelling his dang fool head off, jumping out of bed and throwing his hat in the air."

"That joke's as old as I am," Colt said, "Pay him no mind. Everybody knows he's about three bales short of a haystack."

"Reno," Glenn said, "You'll soon find out there's one big difference between me and Colt."

"What might that be?" Reno asked.

"Colt thinks he's a bull rider and a ladies man, but with me, well…you're looking at the real deal."

"The real deal," Colt repeated.

"That's right," Glenn said. "Old Colt here has eaten so much dirt, they're thinking about incorporating him into the Union…the state of confusion."

"Get settled in," Colt said to Reno as he turned to leave, "Suppers on in about an hour."

The next morning Glenn was showing Reno around the bucking pen. Two bulls were waiting their turn in the chute. "That's Piegow over there and Yetahay behind him," Glenn said, "You want to try your hand?"

"No thank you," Reno said, "I'm too old for that."

"You don't look too old to me," Glenn said. "Where are you from?"

"Missouri, originally," Reno said, "St. Louis."

"I've wanted to see that arch ever since I saw a picture of it," Glenn said.

"What arch?"

"What's it like? Have you ever been up in it?"

"Can't say that I have."

"I understand," Glenn said, "I've lived in Nevada most of my life and I never been to Hoover Dam. Well, not that I remember anyway."

"I left St. Louis as a kid. Right after my mother died."

"Sorry to hear that," Glenn said. "Say, listen. The family is heading up to Heber City for the rodeo this weekend, why don't you come along. You ever been to a rodeo?"

"Not for a long time," Reno replied.

"Well you're in for a treat. Let's put the bucking dummy on these bulls and give 'em a little exercise, then we'll get the dually cleaned up."

"Colt said you were the bucking dummy."

"Yeah, he would," Glenn said. "One of these days, his mouth is going to get his little ass kicked."

"He seems to be a good guy," Reno said.

"One of the best," Glenn said, "But that won't keep me from kicking his little ass."

"Reno's going to Utah with us tomorrow," Glenn said at supper that night.

"That'll be fine," Gordon said, "With me all laid up, you boys may need some help with the bull."

"If you're going with us," Charley said, "We need to do something about your hat."

"What's wrong with my hat? I like it."

"It looks like a reject from an old Cisco Kid rerun," Glenn said.

"Who's the Cisco Kid?" Reno asked.

While Glenn attempted to explain, Charley got up from the table and went to the kitchen counter. Rummaging through a drawer, she finally came out with a tape measure. "Hold still," she said wrapping it around Reno's head.

"What's this for?" Reno asked.

"You'll see."

"I like my hat."

"Yeah, I heard."

That same evening Cassidy got another phone call. "Your Chinese friends didn't do too well, did they?" the voice on the other end said.

"They're not my friends," Cassidy said, "but you're right. They missed a golden opportunity to eliminate the old man. I guess he's tougher than we thought."

"With Teddy out of the way, his estate will be tied up until they find his body. And there may be another way to get rid of Gordon."

"What might that be?"

"Juan Carlos is still in town. He's been looking into the Hobbs' finances."

"Gordon told Ming he had all the money he needed."

"He lied. They're just barely hanging on."

"If Juan could get his hands on that mortgage. . . ."

"Our problems would be over. The old man is counting on his bull to get him to the finals. There will be a big paycheck if Shock Waves can make it to Vegas. If we could somehow prevent that from happening . . . ."

"I think we can handle that," Cassidy said.

"I knew you could. Good night."

"Good night, Senator."

Next morning Reno was in the bunkhouse packing a few things for the trip to Utah. Colt and Glenn were hooking up the trailer and loading the bull. "There you are," Charley said coming through the door.

"Yes ma'am," Reno said, "Just packing my clean shirt."

Charley was carrying a hat box under her arm when she walked up to him. Laying the box on his bunk, she pulled the top off and lifted a brand new black Stetson from the tissue paper wrapping.

"What's this," he asked.

"Just a little present," she replied. Pressing herself against his chest, she placed the hat on his head. "It looks good."

"I like it," Reno said looking in the mirror over her shoulder.

"It's done with a cattleman's crease."

"I appreciate it," he said allowing his hands to slip around the small of her back.

Before he realized she was doing it, Charley unbuttoned the second button on his shirt and reached inside. Drawing out the amulet, she ran her fingers over it. "I can't believe it's ... do you always wear this?"

"Since my mother gave it to me, years ago."

"How long ago was that?"

"More than you can imagine."

Charley raised her eyes up and stared into his. It was as if she was searching for the truth, but expecting a lie, "Were you wearing it that night at Pyramid Lake?"

"What would you know about that?"

"More than you can imagine," she said. Wrapping her fingers in his long hair, she pulled his face down and pressed her mouth to his.

"Well all right then!" Glenn declared coming through the door, "Sorry, I didn't mean to interrupt anything."

"It's all right," Reno said, pulling back from her, "I was just thanking her for my hat. How does it look?"

"A dang sight better than that other thing you been wearing."

"I'll see you boys in a few minutes," Charley said, hiding her reddening face as she headed for the door.

"Thanks again," Reno said after her.

"I'd be careful if I was you," Glenn said when she was gone.

"Careful, about what?"

"Charley."

"She seems nice enough," Reno said.

"It's none of my business," Glenn said, "But after she ran that no-good husband of hers off, she ain't been prone to any romance."

"What's that got to do with me?"

"I'm just saying. If she was to let her guard down and if you were to do her wrong, she'd likely cut your heart out and feed it to the dogs. And believe me she knows how to do it."

"I see what you mean," Reno said, "Thanks for the advice."

The trip to Heber City took all day. It was sundown by the time they got Shock Waves unloaded. Glenn and Colt went to pay their entry fees as Charley and Haley went to arrange for their rooms.

"Glenn and Colt will have this one," Charley said, handing out keys. "Haley and I will be in here, and Reno, you get one all to yourself."

"How come he gets his own private room?" Colt asked.

"There are only two beds in each room," she said, her eyes making contact with Reno's, "I'm sure Reno doesn't want to sleep with either one of you."

"I bet its killing the old man to be sitting at home tonight," Colt said, that evening over supper.

"I'm sure it is," Charley said, "But I promised to keep him updated."

"Will he be all right there all alone?" Haley asked.

"He won't be alone," Charley said. "Some of his old gambling buddies are coming up from Reno. By the time Grandpa takes all their money, they'll be too drunk to drive home. Most of them will spend the night. Deputy John Bull is working tonight. I told him we were having a little trouble with vandals. He promised to keep an eye out for any strange vehicles on the road."

"If any of them Chinamen show up there tonight," Glenn said, "They'll soon find out the old west ain't quite dead yet."

"You're right about that," Colt agreed, "I wouldn't want to take on that bunch of ornery old codgers. They're just looking for a chance to go out in a blaze of glory."

"Beats hell out of dying in a hospital bed with a garden hose shoved up your. . . ."

"I'm trying to eat," Charley said, "Could you please talk about something else?"

"What are you boys going to do tonight, Uncle Colt?" Haley asked.

"We're going down to the Spur Bar and see if we can find any of our friends."

"Can I come?"

"No," Charley said. "Your Uncle Colt's friends can be pretty rowdy and you're too young to be going to any bars."

"What are we going to do?" Haley asked.

"I thought we might take in a movie."

"A movie," Haley repeated, "Do you want to come with us?" she asked turning to Reno.

"He don't want to see some dang tear-jerking girlyfied chick flick," Glenn said, "Reno's coming with us."

"Hey Glenn," Reno said as they were walking down the sidewalk toward the Spur, "what's a chick flick?"

"What's a. . . . Just where, exactly, are you from again?"

"He's putting you on," Colt said, "C'mon, the night is young."

With the rodeo in town, the Spur Bar was jumping. There were all kinds of cowboys, cowboy wannabe's, and the girls that follow them around. Reno had never seen so many attractive young women in one place at the same time. He was thinking the short skirts and tight blouses were a big improvement over what he was used to.

After finding them an empty table, Glenn took a seat against the wall. He was tapping his hands on the table top, keeping time with the blaring jukebox, and grinning like a kid at Christmas. "Boys, this is what rodeo is all about," he said looking around the room.

"Pretty loud," Reno said.

"You boys want a beer?" Glenn asked across the table.

"What?" Colt replied.

"A beer! Do you want a beer?"

"Yeah," Colt said, "I could drink one."

"Good," Glenn said still watching the crowd, "Bring me one too!"

The waitress had just placed the third round of drinks on the table, when a big heavy set cowboy named Posey Nicks hollered across the room at Glenn. "Hey, Rosebud, when's the last time you stayed on a bull for more than eight seconds?"

"When's the last time you had your little ass kicked?" Glenn yelled back.

"Always got to be a smart ass, don't you!" the big man said as he began to walk over to the boys table. Two of his drunken friends followed him.

"Now hold on, Posey," Colt said, "We're just here to have a good time, we don't want no trouble."

"Now that's strange," Posey said turning to his friends, "I heard bull riders were always looking for trouble."

"Is that what you heard?" Glenn said, "Well, I heard you calf ropers wear lace on your pink panties. Course, I never really had any desire to actually find out."

"Why you little son-of-a-bitch," Posey roared, reaching over the table, "I'll show you who wears pink panties." In his exuberance to get to Glenn, the big man lost his balance and toppled over, scattering beer bottles across the table top.

When a couple of them tumbled onto the floor, Glenn reached down to pick one up, but instead of placing it on the table, he smacked the floundering calf roper upside the head with it. The bottle shattered, leaving a ragged cut above Posey's left ear. As the blood began to flow, the calf roper's eyes rolled back in his head, and he went limp as a pole-axed steer.

Seeing the big man suddenly sprawled across the table, his buddies swarmed in to teach Glenn a lesson. Before they could get their hands on the nimble little bull fighter, Glenn went under the table, on his hands and knees, and escaped into the crowd on the dance floor.

With Glenn gone, the calf roper's friends decided to take out their anger on Colt. One of them yanked him to his feet and slugged him. The other one grabbed Reno and attempted to do the same thing, but Reno blocked the punch and delivered a smashing right fist to the attackers face, sending him to the floor for good. With the second man down, Reno grabbed the cowboy who was still beating the slobbers out of Colt, and slugged him.

"I think we need to go!" Reno shouted in Colt's ear as he picked him up by the belt and dragged him toward the door.

Reno and Colt finally made it back to the motel, only to find Glenn propped up in the bed with a six-pack of Coors Light and a bag of powdered doughnuts, watching the Late Show. "Where you boys been?" he asked through his sugar coated mustache, "Colt, where's your front tooth?"

"Somewhere back at the bar, thanks to you…you little…you little. . .." Colt passed out before he could finish.

Reno laid Colt's limp body on the bed, pulled his boots off and covered him with the spread. "See you in the morning," he said to Glenn.

"So long, Reno," Glenn said to Reno's back, "Helluva night," he said cracking open another Coors, "yes sir, helluva night."

Reno was settled in and flipping through channels with his remote when he heard a knock at his door. It was well after midnight and he couldn't imagine who would be out there. After slipping on his jeans he opened the door to find Charley. "You're out late," he said, "Is something wrong?"

"I couldn't sleep. Did I wake you?"

"No, I was still wound up from the bar fight."

"Glenn started it, right?"

"How'd you know?" Reno asked.

"It's his thing. Can I come in?"

"Oh sure, sorry," he said stepping back from the door, "Come on in."

"Haley's asleep and I was still thinking about this morning," she said, running her fingers over the scar on his bare chest, "We...ah...we left a little unfinished business."

"What might that be?"

Charley put her arms around him and once again pressed her mouth to his. This time he pulled her in to him and returned her kiss. Charley was only wearing a t-shirt and jeans. He could feel the firm curves of her breasts as she pressed them against him. There was a little more of Charley than there had been of Martha, and Reno could feel his heart starting to pound.

"Do you really think this a good idea?" he asked.

Still in his embrace, Charley put her head against his chest. "No, it's a terrible idea, but it's going to happen sooner or later. It might as well be tonight while we can have some privacy."

"That's in short supply at the ranch," he said, "That's for sure."

Charley slipped the t-shirt over her head, pushed him down on the bed and fell on top of him. She kissed him over and over as she unbuckled his belt and pulled the zipper down on his jeans. Reno pushed her over beside him and helped her out of her jeans. It was almost dawn before she fell asleep in his arms.

Reno lay awake and pondered the situation he was in. This was Charley's idea, but he still felt a little guilty for taking part in it. To him it had only been a couple of months since he was in Martha's arms. To Charley's way of thinking, it had been a hundred and forty years.

A little after seven, they were awakened by someone banging on the door. "Oh no!" Charley exclaimed, franticly searching the nightstand for her watch, "What time is it?"

"Huh, I don't know." Reno said, "What's all the racket?"

Charley vaulted out of bed, grabbed her clothes and ran for the bathroom as the banging continued on the door. Reno got his jeans on and went to the door. He yanked it open to find Colt standing there.

"What the devil do you. . . .?"

"Is Charley here?" Colt asked.

"Charley," Reno repeated, "Why would she. . . ."

"Yeah, yeah," Colt said, "Just get her out here. We got big trouble."

"What is it?" Charley asked emerging from the bathroom.

"It's Shock Waves."

"What happened?"

"I don't know, but it ain't good, Glenn's with him, we need you."

"I'm coming," Charley said, grabbing one of Reno's shirts and putting it on over her t-shirt, "I'll get my bag from the truck."

When they got to the barn, they found Glenn in the pen kneeling beside Shock Waves, rubbing the big bull's head. Ordinarily, it would be too dangerous to even be in there with the bull, much less sitting beside him. There was no danger now. The big bull was laboring for every breath and he was foaming at the mouth.

"What happened?" Charley asked opening her bag.

"I think he's been poisoned," Glenn said, "I found him like this just a few minutes ago."

"This is bad," Charley said with her ear to the big bull's side. He's drowning. His lungs are full of fluid." After quickly preparing an injection, she laid her hand along Shock Wave's neck, found the pulsing jugular and plunged the needle in.

"What is that?" Colt asked.

"Atropine...for poisoning."

"Will it save him?"

"I don't know. It may be too late."

Haley arrived just as the needle was withdrawn, "Oh no...oh no!" she kept saying.

"What now?" Glenn asked.

"I don't know," Charley said, "I need to know what he ingested. We need to get him back to the clinic."

140

"There's no way to move him," Glenn said.

"I know," Charley said, "Let me think. . . ."

"Mom, do something," Haley begged.

Before anyone could do anything else, Shock Waves took one last gurgling breath, released it, and relaxed. Glenn was still rubbing the big bull's head as the life went out of his eyes. "Son-of-a-bitch," Charley exclaimed slamming her hand down on the now quiet bull's side, "Son-of-a-bitch!"

"Easy Sis," Colt said, "You did everything you could."

They sat in strained silence for a few moments, unsure of what to say, and unwilling to accept that all their hopes and dreams just died right in front of their eyes. "Okay," Charley finally said, "We need to find out what or who did this."

"How do we do that?" Glenn asked.

"I need samples of his feed, the water in his pail and the bedding on the floor."

"I'll do that," Glenn said.

"Be careful," Charley warned, "Whatever it was that killed him, could easily kill you too."

"Colt," Charley said, "You go find security. Find out who might have been around here last night or early this morning, and find out if any of the other stock is sick."

"I'm on my way," Colt said.

"Reno, we need to find someone with a backhoe or a tractor before the spectators start arriving. I want to take this bull home and find out what happened to him. It might help us figure out if anyone did this deliberately. Haley, you go over this stall very carefully while we're gone. Look for anything that shouldn't be here, anything at all, no matter how small. Put these on and be careful what you pick up."

"What about Gramps?" Haley asked, slipping on the latex gloves.

"I don't want to think about that right now," Charley said, "Let's just get the bull loaded and get out of here."

It took a tractor and ten men to get Shock Waves loaded in the trailer. When they finally started for home, Glenn was driving. Colt was in the front passenger seat. Reno, Charley, and Haley were in the back. After pulling out of the barn, they were almost to the gate when Posey and his two friends walked into their path and blocked the exit.

Glenn stopped as Posey walked up to the driver's door. He had a two-inch gauze pad and some tape over his left ear. "We heard about Shock Waves," he said with his hand on Glenn's shoulder.

"Yeah, it was real bad," Glenn said.

"I'm mighty sorry for your loss, Ms. Charley," Posey said looking in the back seat and removing his hat.

"Thank you, Posey," she said.

"Take care of yourself, Rosebud," Posey said turning to the front seat, "Colt, sorry about the tooth."

"Forget it," Glenn said, "Colt's putting the dentist's kids through college."

"If I hear anything, I'll let you know," Posey said, "If you need me to do anything up here, you know how to reach me."

"We appreciate it," Glenn said, "That's Reno back there in the back seat, you all met last night."

"Oh yeah," Posey said, "Hey Reno, good to know you."

"You too, Posey," Reno replied.

"You all drive safe," one of the others said as Glenn pulled through the gate.

Chapter Eleven: Death on the Devil's Horns

It was sundown, three days later when most of the family was sitting on the porch with Gordon. The old man had been unusually quiet ever since receiving the news about Shock Waves. They were all watching as Charley made her way to the house from the clinic. "You can bury him in the morning," she said to Glenn as she walked up on the porch.

"What was it?" Gordon asked.

"Some kind of Organic Phosphate," Charley said, "Most likely a pesticide, it was in the water."

"How could they have gotten him to drink it?" Colt asked.

"Haley found some traces of course salt in the pen. It wasn't anything we would have given him. I think they removed his water, mixed the salt in with some grain, and waited for him to get thirsty."

"That would have taken hours," Glenn said.

"Somebody went to a lot of trouble to kill that bull," Gordon said, "Somebody who must really hate us, or me."

"There is one bright spot," Charley said.

"What's that," Colt asked.

"We've been taking semen from that old bull for a long time. Shock Waves may be gone, but his offspring will be around for many years."

"It could take several years to raise another champion bull," Gordon said.

"We really have no other choice," Charley said.

Things were quiet around the ranch for a few more days. Nothing more was heard from the wind turbine people. It was Friday afternoon when Glenn came in the bunkhouse and found Reno dressed only in a towel, flicking the light switch up and down. "What in blazes are you doing?" Glenn asked.

"This electricity is just amazing," Reno said, "And, man, I love a hot shower."

"They don't have electricity were you come from?" Glenn asked. "Where the devil was that again?"

"Electricity...sure," Reno said, "Who don't?"

"Say listen, Me and Colt figure the mourning period for old Shock Waves should be just about over. We're going into Sparks tonight and blow off a little steam. You want to go?"

"I could use a trip to town," Reno said, "Count me in."

"You ever been to the Nugget?"

"No, never," Reno replied.

"Then you're in for a good time," Glenn said.

It was a cool foggy evening with a misty rain. The forecast was for clearing before midnight and a stretch of good weather after that. Glenn was sitting in the dually with the engine running and the wipers on when Reno and Colt came out of the bunkhouse. "Please tell me, you ain't really wearing that hat," Glenn said.

"I don't want to get my new one rained on," Reno said, "Besides, what's wrong with this hat?"

"What's wrong? If you don't know by now, I can't tell you."

"He's right," Colt said, "You got a perfectly good hat sitting right inside, I don't see. . . ."

"My hat is just fine," Reno said, "Are we going to town or not?"

When they got close to Sparks, an airliner flew over the highway headed for the Reno airport. "That's an airplane," Reno said looking out the window.

"You don't say," Glenn said, peering up through the windshield, "I'll be doggone."

"Shut up and keep driving," Colt said, "I'd like to get there sometime before daylight."

Reno was amazed when they walked into the Nugget, having never seen so many glittering lights or so many people. High rise buildings and the hustle and bustle of big cities were still awe inspiring to him.

"Come on," Colt said, "I'll buy supper."

Colt was leading them toward the Rotisserie Buffet until Reno grabbed him by the shoulder. He was standing in front of a large glass display case. "What is that?" Reno asked.

"A solid gold rooster," Colt replied.

"A golden rooster," Reno repeated, "That thing's got to be worth a thousand dollars."

"Every bit," Colt said, "Maybe more."

"Reno," Glenn said, pushing his hat back, "Where'd you say you're from again?"

"Did you find enough to eat?" Colt asked when Reno returned to the table with his first plateful.

"A man would have to be pretty hard to please to not like this," Reno said, "I never seen so much food in one place in my life. I don't even know what half this stuff is, but I like it."

"Damn," Colt said, when Glenn returned to the table with a heaping plate of food in each hand, "Where are you planning to put all that?"

"Just making sure, I get your money's worth," Glenn said with a grin.

"Let me warm that up for you," the waiter said as he refilled Reno's coffee cup.

"I could get used to this," Reno said.

"No reason why you shouldn't," Colt said.

Unknown to the boys, a group of men were watching them from across the room. "Do you see who that is?" Ming asked his companions.

"I see him," the big man on his right said.

"Who is it?" Don Chow asked. He was still in town enjoying his company expense account.

"The man with the long hair is the one who attacked us at the Hobbs' ranch," Ming said.

"Who is with him?" Chow asked.

"The younger man is Hobbs' grandson," Ming said, "I don't know the other cowboy."

"Have they received any word on Teddy Hobbs?"

"None," Ming said, "I almost wish they would find him. Maybe that will convince them to sign the leases."

"Maybe we can send them an even stronger message," Chow said.

"What do you mean?"

"When those men leave tonight, follow them. When they are well out of town, kill them."

"Kill them," Ming repeated.

"Yes, all of them," Chow said, "Leave no witnesses. Then we will go to see the old man once again. He can't stand many more losses of his family members. There is great risk in leaving those turbines just sitting on the dock in San Diego. We must get them loaded on trucks and away from there. If we do not begin construction on phase one we could lose the grant money."

"Who's up for a little gambling?" Colt asked when they were finished eating.

"I got a little money," Glenn said.

"I'll sit this one out," Reno said, "But you boys go right ahead."

"What's this game called?" Reno asked when Colt and Glenn were seated at the gaming table.

"Pai Gow," Colt replied.

"Like the bull?" Reno said.

"Not quite," Colt said, "It's a little like Twenty-One."

"Looks too complicated for me," Reno said, "You boys have fun. I'm going to look around."

It was after two before Colt and Glenn managed to lose all their money and decided to call it a night. They found Reno holding a conversation with three leggy flight attendants waiting for the shuttle at the front door.

"What was all that about?" Glenn asked when they were in the parking garage.

"They want to take me for a ride on an airplane," Reno replied, "I told Beckwourth I'd fly over these mountains one day and I'm going to."

"Beckwourth," Glenn repeated.

"Old friend of mine, you wouldn't know him."

"An old friend...from back there...where you're from," Glenn said, scratching his head, "Wherever the hell that. . . ."

"Do you want to drive?" Colt asked holding the keys out to Reno, "Me and Glenn have had a few."

"Are you nuts," Glenn said yanking the keys from Colt's hand. "I ain't drunk, and besides, I drive better drunk any day than Reno does stone-cold sober."

"I can't argue with that," Colt said.

They had just hit the dark and deserted two-lane when Glenn noticed headlights coming up on them from behind. "Somebody's coming on strong," he said, watching their high-beams in the rear view mirror. "I hope it ain't the law. You got any breath mints?"

"Breath mints!" Colt repeated. He was riding shotgun and turned around to look, "Just keep going and act normal."

"I don't think it's the law," Reno said. Reaching under the back seat, he pulled out a double rigged shoulder holster and strapped it on.

"What's that for?" Colt asked.

"I saw one of those Chinese guys again tonight."

"Saw him where?"

"At the Nugget," Reno said. "That could be some of them coming up behind us."

"What do you want me to do?" Glenn asked.

"Nothing," Reno replied, "Keep driving, until we see what they're going to do. It may be nothing."

The speeding vehicle came right up on their bumper and stayed there for a mile or so. "Here we go," Glenn said as the unknown vehicle veered into the other lane and started around them. When it pulled up alongside, they recognized it to be the same black suburban that had been at the ranch. As they watched, the rear passenger's window came down and a man stuck an AK-47 out of it.

Glenn stood on the brakes as a burst of automatic rifle fire shattered the driver's window, the windshield, and raked the hood of the dually. The big F-350 went into a right hand skid as the suburban rocketed on by them. Regaining control, Glenn yanked the wheel to the left and abandoned the pavement. Mud was flying as he plowed through the bar ditch, busted through a four-strand barbed-wire fence and started out across the sagebrush.

"Where in hell...are you going?" Colt yelled as his head bounced off the roof.

"The Devil's Horns," Glenn shouted after killing the headlights, "We'll ditch the truck, and lose them in the dark."

Reno was holding on and watching out the rear window as the suburban came to a sliding halt, spun around in the highway, and came after them, "Here they come!"

"I can't see the road!" Colt yelled.

"There ain't no damn road!" Glenn shouted, "Hold on to your butt!"

Glenn kept the pedal to the floorboard as they began to claw their way up a steep gravel slope. Grudgingly giving in to the pull of gravity, the dually began to lose traction and finally halted. "End of the line, boys!" Glenn shouted, throwing it up in park, "Let's get the hell out o' here!"

Hoping to lose the assassins in the dark, Glenn and Colt jumped out and ran for the top of the mountain. Looking back, Colt saw that Reno was out of the truck, but not running. Grabbing Glenn by the shoulder, he pulled him down behind a little dirt mound and tried to hide.

"What's...he...doing?" Colt asked between heaving breaths.

"We got to...go back," Glenn said.

"Too late...stay down."

They watched as the suburban bounced to a halt and six heavily armed gunmen piled out. They appeared to be some of the same men who had been at the ranch. Reno was illuminated in the headlights but made no attempt to run.

"It seems your friends have abandoned you," Ming said.

"I don't need them," Reno said, letting his hat fall back to his shoulders.

"You are a talented student of Changquan. I am curious to know with whom you studied."

148

"A dear friend, long ago."

"Too bad it will be of no use to you now," Ming said, "We are going to kill you the modern way."

"You won't kill me," Reno said, "But that won't keep me from killing all of you."

"You are a brave man, but very foolish," Ming said.

Glenn and Colt watched in horror as Reno reached around his chest with both hands and drew twin Berettas. The staccato of crackling gunfire erupted in the quiet desert night as dozens of shots were fired. Bullets were shredding the sagebrush and kicking up little plumes of dirt surrounding Colt and Glenn as they huddled together behind their earthen sanctuary.

"We got to get out of here," Glenn whispered when the shooting finally ended, "They'll be after us next."

"What about Reno?"

"There's nothing we can do for him."

"All right," Colt said, "I'm right behind you, let's go!" The two of them jumped to their feet and began to flee into the night.

"Where are you all going?" a familiar voice asked.

Spinning around, Colt saw Reno standing at the side of the dually. "We thought...ah...how did you...are they all. . . ."

"The fights over," Reno said, "they lost."

Trying to catch his breath, Glenn sagged to the ground, "That's the first time anybody ever tried to kill me," he said, wiping his forehead, "That was a damn nightmare."

"Glenn," Reno said, "You think you can get off your butt long enough to back the truck down out of here and get it turned around?"

"Yeah, I can do that," Glenn said, getting to his feet. He had to back down over two hundred yards before he got to a spot level enough to turn the truck around. When he was finally headed in the right direction, he blew the horn."

"Let's go," Colt said.

"Where's the gas tank on this thing?" Reno asked, looking at the suburban.

"Underneath," Colt said, "In the back."

Reno knelt down and fired two shots into the tank. When the gas began to pour out, he removed a match from his pocket and struck it on his belt-buckle. "Now let's go," he said with a grin and tossed the match under the suburban. The burning suburban was casting an eerie flickering glow on the Devil's Horns as they made their way back to the highway and sped away into the night.

Next morning, Gordon was wound up and ready to bring down the thunder when the three occupants of the bunkhouse walked in for breakfast. Charley was sitting opposite the old man waiting for the war to start. "I want to know just one damn thing," Gordon said.

"What's that?" Colt asked through blood-shot eyes.

"Did anybody survive the wreck my truck was in? Most of the glass is gone, the grill is stuffed with sagebrush, and it looks like a sieve. I don't know how you managed to drive it back here."

"The damn thing's built Ford tough," Glenn said.

"I'll get to you in a minute, Rosebud," Gordon stormed, "Right now, I want a straight answer!"

"It was Reno," Glenn blurted out, "Me and Colt were hiding in the brush."

"What is he talking about?" Gordon asked.

"Those Chinese men that were here the other day," Reno said.

"What about them?"

"Six of them ran us off the road this morning and tried to kill us."

"Kill you!" Charley said.

"Those bullet holes in the truck are from the gun fight," Colt said.

"Gun fight!" Charley exclaimed, "Are you serious, they were actually shooting at you?"

"Yeah," Glenn said, "If it hadn't been for Reno, they probably would've gotten us. He killed every damn one of 'em."

"Killed them," Charley repeated turning to Reno, "I can't believe this kind of thing is happening around here. None of you were hurt?"

"We're fine," Reno said, "But there are some bad people running around here right now and they may not be finished with you."

"We have to call the sheriff," Charley said.

"I wouldn't do that," Reno said.

"Why not," Gordon asked.

"They followed us from the Nugget last night. Those men knew who we were and they intended to kill us, there's no doubt about that. It was meant to be a message to you about those damn wind turbines. Whoever sent those assassins won't report them missing, I promise you. They would have to answer too many questions about what they're doing around here."

"Then what do we do?" Gordon asked.

"Nothing," Reno said. "Hopefully, whoever sent them will finally figure out that you can't be bluffed, and they'll leave you alone."

"And if they don't?" Charley asked.

"We'll deal with that when it comes," Reno said, "In the mean time, I would make sure someone takes Haley to school."

"I'm keeping her out of school for awhile," Charley said.

"That's probably a good idea," Reno said, "Neither of you should be out on the roads alone."

"They won't be," Gordon said.

Colt and Glenn were walking back to the bunkhouse while Reno went to check on his horse. "Did you see anything weird out there last night?" Glenn asked.

"You mean beside half-a-dozen raving Chinamen trying to blow our heads off?"

"Yeah," Glenn said, "besides that."

"Are you talking about Reno's eyes right after the gunfight?"

"Exactly," Glenn said, "Then you seen 'em too?"

"I didn't see a damn thing," Colt said.

"Yeah, me neither."

Late the next afternoon, a sheriff's patrol car pulled up in the yard. "Evening," the deputy said as he got out.

"Evening, John," Gordon said, "Come on up and have a seat." John Bull was a Washoe County Deputy Sheriff.

Colt and Charley came out when they heard Gordon talking. "Ms. Hobbs, Colt," John said.

"What can I do for you?" Gordon asked.

"A local land owner called us this morning. He found his fence torn down and a burned out suburban up near the Devil's Horns."

"That's strange," Charley said.

"It gets stranger," John said. "There were enough automatic weapons up there to equip a small army."

"You don't say," Gordon said.

"Yes sir, and at least a hundred spent shell casings scattered around, along with six very dead Chinese guys."

"Dead," Charley repeated.

"And they were mutilated, so to speak," John said, "Some of their private parts, begging your pardon, Ms. Hobbs. Evidently, they were up there for a couple of nights."

"What about their private parts?" Charley asked.

"They were missing," John said, "Along with some of their faces and hands."

"So what exactly do you want from me?" Gordon asked.

"The sheriff wanted us to check with the people in the area to see if anybody knew anything about it."

"John, considering the shape my leg is in, if you're asking did I cut the nuts off a bunch of Chinese gun runners and leave their dead asses up on the Devil's Horns, I'd have to say no."

"No, I didn't mean to imply. I think the coyotes did most of the damage to their bodies."

"Sounds reasonable to me," Gordon said.

"Well, all right then" John said, after an uncomfortable pause, "Thanks anyway. You all have a nice evening."

"You too, John," Gordon said, "Come back anytime."

Reno waited to walk up on the porch until the deputy was gone, "What did he want?"

"They found the men that tried to kill you," Charley said.

"Do they know we were involved?"

"It didn't appear that way to me," Charley said.

"You were right about one thing," Gordon said, "The law doesn't have a clue who those men were or what they were doing around here."

"I'm not surprised," Reno said, "Whoever hired them wants to avoid any connection to them."

"Charley," Gordon said, "Would you give us a minute?"

Charley was curious, but respectful of Gordon's wishes. "Of course," she said turning to go inside, "I'll call you when supper's on."

"You know, Reno," Gordon said when Charley was gone, "I been doing a lot of thinking while I've been laid up."

"What about?"

"This ranch and all the trouble we're in. Of course, we've had trouble before, but this seems different somehow. The poor economy, folks who want to work can't find a decent job. And the damn gas prices, it's like its all being run by somebody, somewhere, but nobody knows who."

"I don't follow you."

"Back in the thirties, we had the great depression. I was just a kid, but I remember it well. My dad couldn't afford any hired help. I quit school in the tenth grade and worked the ranch full time. It was hell, but we got through it. Then came the war, it was bad, especially right after Pearl Harbor, but it was different somehow."

"Different…how so?"

"The whole country went to war. I joined the army and went to Europe, but even the folks back here were in the fight. Scrap drives, war bonds, rationing and victory gardens. Detroit stopped building automobiles and started building tanks, jeeps, and bombers. The whole damn country rolled up their sleeves and won that war."

"Now days, you can't find two political or cultural groups that will agree on anything. It's like we're three different countries anymore. Some people expect the government to supply everything they need while they basically sit on their ass. There's the politicians who want to spend every damn dime we have and borrow even more. And then there's the rest of us, who just want the government to leave us the hell alone."

"I suppose you got a point," Reno said.

"I wish there were more men like you. Take the bull by the horns and make no apology for doing it."

"It may be a little easier for me," Reno said, "I don't have the responsibilities of taking care of anyone but myself."

Come inside," Gordon said, "I want to show you something. Hand me that damn cane, if you will."

After finally getting to his feet, the old man led Reno into the den. It was a dark manly room with lots of natural wood and stone. There were three old saddles carefully placed on stands along the wall and a case full of old long guns. Gordon went to the gun case and after some effort, pulled the bottom drawer open.

Still balanced on his cane, he removed an old two gun rig from its protective wraps and pulled one of the twin revolvers from the holster. "You ever seen one of these?" Gordon asked, handing the old thumb buster to Reno.

"I don't believe it...I mean...I have, as a matter of fact." Reno rubbed his hands over the old revolver and thought about how many times he had drawn and fired it. He wanted to tell Gordon all about the formidable weapon, but he held back. Pulling the hammer to half-cock, he spun the cylinder, "Just like new."

"I keep 'em cleaned and oiled. Next to my family and this ranch, they're my prized possessions. They belonged to the Reno Kid. Jonas Hobbs', my great grandfather, got them from the sheriff after the Kid was hanged, or not hanged, or whatever the hell happened to him."

"Are they worth anything these days?"

"Son, these old dragoons are damn near priceless, but I wouldn't sell 'em. Even if it meant I had to live in a tent the rest of my life."

"I'm glad they're in good hands," Reno said.

"I thought you would be," Gordon said, "There's something I've been meaning to ask you." The old man stood quietly as he carefully chose his words, "Reno, I know who you are. At least I think I do, or maybe I'm just a crazy old man, but. . . ."

"C'mon, boys!" Charley yelled from the kitchen, "Supper's on the table!"

"Let's eat," Gordon said, "We'll talk later." After, carefully replacing the dragoon in its case, he closed the drawer.

Finally, after almost a month, the dreaded news came about Teddy. Some back-country hikers found the wreckage and reported it to the Forest Service. The NTSB dropped a team in by helicopter, did a quick survey, and recovered Teddy's scattered remains.

The memorial service was hard on the family, but having at least part of Teddy to bury seemed to bring them some closure.

It was several days after the funeral that Clark Brown showed up at the ranch. "Clark, what brings you out here?" Gordon asked.

"Mr. Hobbs, I got something on my mind and I want to run it by you."

"Well come on up on the porch and let's talk."

Colt and Reno were working in the barn when they saw Clark drive up. They joined the group on the porch just after Charley came out of the house. "You all know Clark Brown from the airport," Gordon said.

"Yes," Charley said, "Clark, how are you?"

"I'm fine, Ms. Hobbs, just fine."

"Clark," Gordon said, "This is Reno. He's new around here."

"Good to meet you, Reno," Clark said.

"All right," Gordon said, "What's on your mind."

"I've managed to get my hands on the preliminary report from Teddy's crash."

"I thought those things were secret until the NTSB released them to the public," Charley said.

"Yeah, they are," Clark replied, "But I've got a friend, who has a friend."

"What does the report say?" Colt asked.

"Something about this stinks," Clark said, "This investigation has just died. There has been no follow up. It's all over as far as I can tell."

"What stinks about it?" Charley asked.

"The investigator on the site thinks the crash was caused by catastrophic engine failure. He said it appeared to have been a sudden loss of oil pressure that brought Teddy down, but no one is looking into it."

"What do you think?" Gordon asked.

"That airplane was equipped with two 600 horsepower Merlin Turbo-Prop engines. It is unlikely that either of them lost oil pressure, but both of them at the same time, it's impossible. Mr. Hobbs, I think Teddy was murdered and somebody in the NTSB is covering it up."

"NTSB," Gordon repeated, "That's the federal government, right?"

"Yes sir," Clark said.

"That dirty son-of-a-bitch," Gordon whispered.

"Who's that?" Charley said.

"How can we prove any of that?" Colt asked before Gordon could answer.

"I need to get to the wreckage."

"Do you know where it is?" Colt asked.

"I've got the coordinates," Clark said, unfolding a map.

"The what?" Reno asked, looking over Clark's shoulder.

"Coordinates," Clark repeated, "You know, the GPS location."

"This is the Feather River, isn't it?" Reno asked pointing to the wavy blue line on map.

"Yes, but there's no way to drive in there," Clark said, "The crash site is many miles away from there, in some really rough country. We'll have to go on foot."

"Or horseback," Reno said.

"Do you know that country?" Gordon asked.

"Sure," Reno said, "I've been all over up there, looking for Jim Beck. . . ."

"Jim who," Gordon said.

"A friend," Reno said, "You wouldn't know him. These lines here," he asked Clark, "Are they roads?"

"Yeah," Clark said. "Haven't you ever seen a map before?"

"This line that ends in the green area, do you know where that is?" Reno asked.

"Angels Pass," Clark said, "I'm pretty sure we can get close to it."

"All right then," Reno said, "We'll drive up to there and take the horses the rest of the way."

"What about the truck and trailer?" Colt asked.

"I'm not sure," Reno said, "We may not come back out the same way."

"I'll go along and drive the truck back," Charley offered, "You can call us to meet you wherever you end up."

"All right," Colt said, "Clark, be back here at daylight."

"I'm staying right here," Clark said, "My gear's in the car."

In spite of losing Ming and his henchmen, Juan Carlos and Don Chow were still in Reno, determined to see the project through. They were sitting in the lobby of the Nugget Casino waiting on Will Cassidy when Juan's cell phone rang. "Hello," Juan said.

"Juan Carlos," the voice on the other end said.

"Yes, Senator, what is it?"

"We got big trouble."

"What kind of trouble?"

"My people intercepted an encrypted email to a NTSB inspector in Las Vegas. That damn Clark Brown got his hands on the NTSB report for the Hobbs crash. I sent some men down to his office, but the place is locked up tight and he's nowhere to be found. I think Brown is going to try and find the crash site. He'll probably get some of the Hobbs' family to help him."

"What do you want me to do?"

"Most of those damn Chinamen are dead and the rest don't know one end of a horse from the other. I want you to get some of Rollo's boys and get up there after Clark and whoever is with him. You Mexicans are all cowboys, right?"

"I suppose," Juan said.

"Good, you won't have any trouble getting into the back country."

"How will Rollo's men know where to look?"

"I'll text you the GPS numbers as soon as I get them. Tell those men, I don't want Brown or any of the men with him to make it to that crash site, and I damn sure don't want any of them coming out of there. That's remote, rugged country up there, tell them to take plenty of gear, they may be in there for a while. And tell them to take plenty of fire power. The men from the Reno Kid Ranch are likely the ones who killed Ming. Don't take any chances. As soon as your men find the Hobbs', kill them all. This has to end, right now."

"Where can we get that many horses and the equipment we'll need?"

"Tell 'em to go by my ranch, I'll have my people get everything ready."

"What about a guide to get them in there?"

"He'll be waiting at the ranch."

"I understand," Juan Carlos said, "Don't worry. Rollo's men will not fail."

"They better not."

"You all promise me that you'll be careful," Charley said to the men as they loaded the horses.

"I'll try and let you know what's going on," Colt said. "The reception up there is pretty bad, so it may be several days before you hear from us."

Gordon came out to the yard and spoke to them. He was still using the cane but getting around better every day. "I wish I was going with you boys," he said.

"Me too, Grandpa," Colt said, "With these horses, I feel like we're back in the old days with Grandpa Clay and the Reno Kid."

"Son" the old man said, "You may be closer to the Reno Kid than you could possibly ever imagine."

"Well, Reno Kid or not," Colt said, "Nobody's going to keep us from that crash site."

"You sound more like Clay Hobbs all the time," Gordon said, "I'm mighty proud of you."

"Thanks, Grandpa. That means a lot."

"Reno," the old man said, "After that deal with the Chinese, I have a bad feeling you boys may not be alone up there. I want you to take plenty of guns. That's wild country and you'll be on your own. There are bad people involved in this and I think they're getting desperate."

Reno gave him a smile and pulled back his duster, exposing twin Beretta's tucked into a double-rigged shoulder holster. Colt was wearing an old .45 revolver, and he had a bolt action 30-06 in his saddle scabbard. Clark had a Glock 9mm and a worn 30-30 in his saddle scabbard.

Glenn was wearing an ancient six gun, but carrying a brand new Chinese AK-47. "Souvenir," he said with a grin.

"You got any ammo for that?" Colt asked.

"Bout three-hundred rounds," Glenn said patting his saddle bag, "Give or take."

"I see you boys are way ahead of me," Gordon said, "but, I want you to take this." He handed a black 870 tactical shotgun to Reno.

"Thanks" Reno said, slinging it over his shoulder, "It's a shotgun, right."

"That's right," Gordon said, "There are seven rounds of buckshot in there. The safety is at the top of the trigger guard. Push in on the safety, yank the trigger and work the pump, its hell at close range."

"All right, boys" Colt said, "Load up. We got a long way to go."

The drive to the Sierras took all day. Toward the end of their journey, they were traveling on a narrow and winding dirt road. Dusk was fast approaching as Charley stopped by the entrance to a primitive Forest Service fire trail. "This road is getting really narrow," she said, "This may be the last place we come to that's wide enough to turn this thing around."

"I think you're right," Colt said. "Back it in there and we'll unload the animals."

"Please be careful," she said when all the stock was finally on the ground.

"We will," Colt assured her.

Charley went to Reno's side and put her arms around his neck. "I don't know what we would have done if you hadn't come along," she whispered.

"I'm glad you feel that way," Reno said. Letting his sombrero fall back on his shoulders, he put his arms around her waist.

"Take care of this bunch and bring them home safe," she whispered, "When you get back, we need to have a long talk."

"We will," he said, "and you be careful going home."

"I'm going to stop at the first motel I can find and spend the night. I wish you were. . . ."

"That's a good idea, Sis," Colt said from the saddle, "We'll be seeing you. C'mon Reno."

Mounting his horse, Reno followed Colt toward the timber. "Reno," Charley said to his back.

"Yes ma'am," he said turning in the saddle.

"I still think that's the ugliest hat I ever saw."

"Yes ma'am," he said turning back to the trail, "Thank you ma'am."

"It's Charley, dammit, Charley!" she yelled after him.

Charley stood in the road and watched until they were swallowed up by the dark timber. Her mind was racing with the seemingly impossible situation she was experiencing. She scarcely dared to think about what she was feeling. Could it be even remotely possible, that an old curse of unrequited love was being revisited on yet another strong Hobbs woman?

The four searchers were several miles from the road when darkness descended on the Sierras and Reno called a halt. "This should be far enough in. We shouldn't draw anyone's attention from here," he said. "We'll stay the night, and head out again at first light."

The searchers had two pack mules with them that carried some basic camping gear and extra feed and hobbles for the horses. It wasn't long before they had a simple, but comfortable camp set up. After supper, they were relaxing around the fire.

"I sort o' like this," Colt said to Reno, "I guess you've been doing this for awhile."

"Most of my life," Reno replied.

"You wouldn't last a week out here," Glenn said. He was stretched out by the fire with his head on a saddle and his hat over his face.

"I could be a mountain man," Colt said, "As long as I had electricity and running water."

"And a dentist," Glenn said, "Don't forget the dentist."

"Why did we bring him along?" Colt asked.

"Cause he's the real deal," Reno said.

"Damn right," Glenn agreed from under his hat.

The sun was just up when they broke out over Angel's Pass. It was going to be a hot clear day. Clark was checking his GPS unit. "Which way," Reno asked.

"Northwest," Clark replied, indicating their direction of travel with his arm.

"I believe we'll have to go west a spell and then cut back north," Reno said. "That's some pretty steep country down through there."

"Lead on," Colt said, "You're the mountain man."

Charley spent the night in Cisco. She was filling up at a station alongside I-80 when she noticed three pickups pull in. Two of the trucks were towing gooseneck stock trailers. There were at least a dozen horses in all. Most of the men getting out of the trucks appeared to be Latino. Some of them were cowboy types, but a few of the others seemed to be strangely dressed for a trail ride.

Deciding it was really none of her business what they were dressed for, Charley replaced the gas cap, got in the truck, and headed out toward the eastbound ramp and Reno. Just before pulling out of the gas station, she noticed the name of a ranch painted on the side of one of the pickups and the man standing beside it.

As soon as she was on the interstate, she fished out her phone and tried to call Colt. "Come on...come on," she said listening to the endless ringing. Finally she was routed to Colt's voice mail. "Colt, listen," she said after the beep, "One of Reed Henry's pickups is sitting down here on the interstate at Cisco. Whoever's driving it is with a rough looking bunch of Mexicans and two trailer loads of horses. I may be paranoid, but Will Cassidy is with them, they could be coming after you. Call me when you get this."

"Where are we going?" Cruz asked the cowboy who had been driving the first pickup. The two of them were going over a map laid out over the hood. Cruz Portillo was the lead henchman for the expedition.

"According to these GPS numbers, the wreckage is down in the National Forest, northwest of here."

"How close can we get in the trucks?" Cassidy asked.

"Right about here," the cowboy said, pointing to the map. Parnell Fisher was the wilderness guide Reed Henry hired to get Juan Carlos' men to the crash site.

"We will still have a long way to go." Cruz said.

"Yep," Parnell said, "we'll make it all right, but there's one thing."

"And that is?"

"I'm just the wrangler on this varmint hunt. If there's any shooting, I'm not getting involved."

"You just get us there," Cruz said, "We'll take care of the varmints."

"You may have your hands full," Parnell warned, "Gordon Hobbs never raised any cowards."

"We shall see," Cruz said.

"Cassidy," Parnell asked, "What's your interest in all this?"

"The Senator asked me to come along."

"I never knew you to be a cowboy," Parnell said, "Can you manage this trip?"

"The Cassidy's were cowboys all the way back to my great-grandfather, I'm told. I'm just another chip off the same old block."

It was after noon by the time Parnell got to the trailhead at Shirt Tail Canyon. It took another two hours to get everything loaded and ready to go. In spite of what Juan Carlos had told Reed Henry, half of this bunch couldn't even saddle their own horse.

Parnell had no way of knowing, but he was twenty-five miles from where Reno and his men had entered the forest. Unfortunately for Reno, Parnell was an experienced guide. Both groups were headed for a violent rendezvous.

Chapter Twelve: Battle at Gunstock Pass

The next afternoon, the searchers topped out on a high mountain ridgeline and Colt's cell phone rang. "It's a message from Charley," he said, flipping the phone open and pressing it to his ear. "The signal's weak. I can barely make it out." After losing the signal completely, Colt closed it up and put it back in his pocket.

"What did she say?" Reno asked.

"She was on the road yesterday morning when she saw a group of men with horses."

"And," Glenn said.

"She thinks they may be coming after us."

"Why would she think that?" Glenn asked.

"If Charley thinks they're after us," Reno said, "I'd say there's a good chance they probably are."

"I'd say that's right," Colt said, "Especially since they're driving trucks from Reed Henry's ranch and Will Cassidy is with them."

"Cassidy," Reno repeated, "Any relation to Wilbur Cassidy?"

"Great-grandson, I believe," Colt said.

"I'll be damned," Reno said.

"You know Wilbur Cassidy?" Glenn asked.

"I know him," Reno said, "I mean, no, how could I know him? I meant to say I know of him."

"I just thought he might be from back there...where you're from," Glenn said, "Wherever the hell that is."

"We need to find some grass for these horses," Reno said, unwilling to engage Glenn in another debate, "It'll be dark soon."

They were entering a small isolated valley just at sundown when Reno spotted a black tail doe feeding at the edge of the timber. He pulled up on his horse and turned to Clark, "Let me borrow your rifle," he said.

Before Colt could ask what he was doing, Reno worked the lever and fired. The deer jumped straight up in the air and ran into the trees. "It's a good thing you missed," Colt said, "It ain't deer season."

"Yeah," Clark said, "That was too far for that old 30-30."

"I didn't miss," Reno said, handing the rifle back to Clark, "What's a deer season?"

"You can't just shoot a deer whenever you want," Clark said.

"I believe I just did," Reno said. "I don't know what that stuff was you fed me last night, but we're having real meat tonight. C'mon let's make camp."

"It was freeze-dried…beef stroganoff," Clark said turning his horse to follow Reno, "It's the latest thing in trail food."

"It was pretty bad," Glenn said, "I was burping the damn stuff all night."

"I hate to tell you this," Clark said to Glenn, "but you're going to be burping it again tonight, that deer ran off."

"She's right inside the trees," Reno said over his shoulder.

"Some people just can't admit it when they're wrong," Clark mumbled.

Just as Reno predicted, the deer, shot through both lungs, expired just beyond the tree line. He was standing over her when the rest arrived. "Not too dang bad for an old 30-30," Glenn said to Clark.

"All right," Clark said with a grin, "I admit it, I was wrong."

The rest set up camp while Reno gutted and skinned the deer. It wasn't long before he had the back straps and six big steaks roasting over the fire.

"I believe that's the best steak I ever put in my mouth," Glenn said, while they were eating, "Where'd you learn to cook like that?"

"My mother taught me, mostly," Reno said.

"I have to admit," Clark said, "this is mighty fine."

"How far from the crash site, you figure we are?" Reno asked.

"As the crow flies, it's another ten or twelve miles," Clark said, "At the rate we've been going, we should be there late tomorrow or first thing the next day for sure."

"I don't think we should take these horses anywhere near it," Reno said.

"Why not," Colt asked.

"If Cassidy is with those men, it's probably safe to say they know where the crash site is as well as we do."

"That's probably right." Clark said. "Whoever sent them would have told them where to look."

"Then we need to set up a base camp several miles away and up in some high remote country," Reno said.

"That's a good idea," Colt said, "If those men with Cassidy don't know where we are, they can't ride right up on us."

"That's right," Reno said, "We can go to the site on foot. Then we'll poke around and try to find out who else is up here with us."

"What if they show up at the crash site?" Glenn asked.

"It's going to be real hard on their mothers," Reno replied.

"I know that's right," Glenn said.

"What do you mean? Clark asked, "What's their mothers got to do with this?"

"Reno's right," Colt said, "I'm tired of running from this bunch. After what they tried to do to us out on the road, they best not even think about showing themselves up here."

"Get some sleep boys," Reno said, "We're out of here at first light."

Just before sundown the next afternoon, the searchers were on a ridgeline looking down into a deep rugged canyon. "This is Gunstock Pass," Reno said.

"How do you know?" Glen asked.

"I've been here before," Reno said, "A long time ago."

"It should be right around here," Clark said. "This is the spot."

"Look...down there," Colt said, pointing down the slope, "Broken trees, and they look fresh."

"That's it," Clark said.

"Leave the horses up here," Reno said, "Let's go take a look."

It wasn't long before they located the scattered wreckage in the trees. Clark was searching for pieces of the main fuselage. After finding what he was looking for, he began to examine it with a magnifying glass. "This is it," he said, "Proof positive."

"What is it?" Colt asked.

"This is the spot where the oil lines would have been close to each other. See the burned spot on the metal?"

"I see it," Colt said.

"They used some kind of small explosive charge to sever the oil lines. The engines would have failed moments later. The hot oil probably caught fire and filled the cabin with heat and smoke. Teddy was going down and there was nothing he could do about it. He was probably unconscious before it ever hit."

Colt was sitting quietly and staring off into space. "I'm sorry, Colt," Clark said, "I forgot for a moment Teddy was your father. This must be hard for you."

"It's all right," Colt said, "What about the locator beacon?"

"They must have removed it in Sacramento. Those things are practically indestructible. If it was here, it would have gone off."

"You boys keep working," Reno said, "I'm going to check our back-trail and try to find a water source so we can set up camp."

"I'm going with Reno," Glenn said.

Reno started up the slope but turned back, "We'll be back before sundown, but keep your eyes open."

Reno and Glenn traveled two ridges over, before finding an isolated little mountain meadow with plenty of grazing for the animals. There was just a trickle of snow-melt water from a high country spring, but it was enough to supply them with what they needed. The secluded campsite was three miles from the crash site. Reno figured that would be far enough to prevent anyone snooping around the wreckage from knowing where they were camped.

Reno and Glenn rode back to the crash site just as darkness began to fall. "Are you boy's ready?" he asked after locating Colt and Clark.

"Just about," Colt said.

"I need to come back with some tools in the morning," Clark said, "We found both engines. I want to get a couple of key parts out of each one of them and a few other things. The NTSB will have to listen to us when we bring all this evidence back."

"So you think someone killed Teddy?" Glenn asked.

"This was no accident," Clark said, "It was well planned by someone who knew what they were doing."

Later that night, they were relaxed around the camp fire. "How long will we be up here?" Reno asked.

"Give me tomorrow," Clark said. "I want to gather as much evidence as that mule can carry, and I want to shoot as many pictures and video as possible. We should be ready to go first thing the next day."

"While you and Colt are at the crash site, Glenn and I are going to poke around and find out where Cassidy and his men might be."

"I think that's a good idea," Colt said. "If they're coming after us, it would be nice to have a little warning."

Ten miles away, Cassidy, Parnell, and Cruz were sitting by another campfire. There were nine other men with them. Most of them were rump sprung and saddle sore. "How much farther is this cursed place we are going?" Cruz asked.

"Be there by noon tomorrow," Parnell advised, "Can't be more than ten or twelve miles. You boys ain't getting tired are you? It's only our second day."

"I'm beginning to think you don't know where we are," Cruz said.

"If that's how you feel," Parnell said, "I'll head out at dawn and you can find your own way from here."

"Do not presume to play with me," Cruz said, "I am here to kill some gringos, one more won't matter."

Before Cruz even knew Parnell was moving, there was a Colt .45 in the old guide's hand, the hammer was cocked and it was pointed at the end of Cruz's nose. "I'll tell you one damn thing," Parnell warned, "Some of us gringos require a little more killing than you may be used to."

An instant later, the rest of Cruz's men were on their feet holding guns on Parnell. Still looking down the barrel of the .45, Cruz motioned for them to sit down. Realizing he still very much needed Parnell, and not anxious to test him, Cruz backed down, "I am tired, my friend. I meant no offense."

"None taken," Parnell said dropping the hammer and holstering his Colt.

"What was that?" Cassidy asked staring out into the surrounding darkness.

"I didn't hear it," Parnell said.

"There...there it is again," Cassidy said.

"You are hearing things," Cruz said, "There is nothing up here to be afraid of."

"That's not exactly true," Parnell said.

"What do you mean?" Cassidy asked.

"The bleeding heart do-gooders got lion hunting outlawed years ago, and now the damn cats up here are thick as liars at a political convention and they ain't scared of people anymore. It's not a good idea to be running around up here alone. Especially for small people, you know like women and kids."

"El Tigre," Cruz said.

"No," Parnell said. "We're too far north for jaguars. These cats are puma's you know cougars, mountain lions."

"Could one of them be out there right now?" Cassidy asked.

"If there was a cougar around, the horses would let us know in a hurry," Parnell said.

"Hello in the camp!" a stranger shouted from the darkness.

"Who could that be?" Cassidy asked.

"I don't know," Parnell said, "But you better hide them guns."

"Saw your fire. Thought we'd stop by!" the voice shouted.

"Come on in and welcome," Parnell said.

Two figures rode out of the darkness and got off their horses. One was a man in his late thirties. The other seemed to be a woman, barely twenty years old. "I'm Tom Cooper," the man said, "U.S. Forest Service. This is one of my summer interns, Karen Gilstrap."

"Good to know you both," Parnell said, "Sit down, have a cup of coffee. What are you doing way up here in the middle of the night?"

"The rangers over in district seven spotted some vehicles parked at the Shirt Tail Canyon trailhead."

"Yep, they're ours, what of it?"

"There are no back country permits currently issued for this part of the forest," Karen said.

"And no one is licensed to conduct trail rides in the back country," Tom said.

"Well," Parnell said, "I'm sure my boss said the paper work was all in order when he sent us up here."

"Who might your boss be?" Tom asked.

Without waiting for Parnell to answer, Cassidy broke into the conversation, "I'm Will Cassidy," he said, "Chairman of the Nevada Alternative Energy Commission."

"Glad to meet you Mr. Cassidy," Tom said, "but you know you're in California, right?"

"Well yes, but I . . . ."

"I work for Senator Reed Henry," Parnell said. "He set up this shindig."

"U.S. Senator Henry?"

"That's the one," Parnell said.

"That makes it even worse," Tom said with a grin.

"Why's that?" Cassidy nervously asked.

"I'm a Republican," Tom replied.

"I don't see where that. . . ."

"I'm only kidding," Tom said before Cassidy could finish. "I'm not going to write any citations, but you men will have to pack up and head back toward your trucks first thing in the morning."

"Perhaps this will help," Cruz said, reaching into his coat.

"No!" Parnell shouted, but he was too late. Cruz pulled a Glock out of his shoulder holster and began firing at the startled rangers. Unable to escape, both Tom and Karen were hit multiple times.

When they were on the ground, Cruz got to his feet and went to inspect the bodies. Tom was dead when Cruz rolled him over, but Karen was still alive. Bleeding badly from her nose and mouth, the gutsy intern was struggling to reach her cell phone. Before she could get hold of it, the brutal Mexican killer placed the Glock against her temple and pulled the trigger.

"What the hell?" Parnell shouted.

"That...that wasn't. . . . ." Cassidy was in shock, having never witnessed a murder before. He grabbed his mouth and ran for the darkness.

"We have no time for delays," Cruz said, "We must get to the crash site, kill Clark Brown and anybody with him and get out of here. I am sick of this camping out nonsense and I need a shower. At first light we go, now get some sleep."

The forest service horses weren't picketed. When the shooting started, they bolted. It would take them all night and the next day, but they were headed home. It wouldn't be long before a search would be mounted to find Tom and Karen.

Early next morning, Colt and Clark went back to the crash site. They left their horses in camp, thinking it would be easier to hide if anyone showed up. Reno and Glenn took their horses and rode off down their back-trail, to see if anyone was following them.

Just after eleven, Glenn was riding in front of Reno when the bark on a pine tree, just off to his left, exploded. The sound of the shot arrived a moment later. The two of them spurred the horses into some dense timber and dismounted.

"Damn," Glenn said, peeking around a pine tree, "That was close."

"Did you see 'em?" Reno asked.

"No, too far away."

"Leave the horses," Reno said, "We'll go after them on foot." Glenn untied the AK-47 from behind his saddle and followed Reno down the hill. Being careful to stay in the trees, the two of them began to close the distance to their attackers.

"Do you know how to shoot that thing?" Reno asked.

"We'll see."

After noticing some movement in the rocks down below, Reno grabbed Glenn by the shirt and pulled him down, "There's two of them," he said, "Right down there in the rocks."

"I see 'em," Glenn said, spying the two men watching over top of a big boulder. There was a scope-sighted sniper rifle sitting on a bipod in front of them.

"Stay here," Reno said, "I'm going to get around behind them."

"I ain't scared of this bunch," Glenn said.

"Never figured you were. I need you to keep watch. If any more of them show up, let me know."

"How do I do that?"

"Shoot 'em."

"Wait a minute," Glenn said, grabbing Reno's coat, "We ain't playing here are we? This is the real deal."

"It's never going be any more real," Reno said, "Take care of yourself. Remember, it's them or us."

Glenn was watching the snipers intently and waiting for Reno to get to them, when he was startled by a soft noise behind him. "All right, Gringo," a voice behind him said, "Drop your rifle and stand up."

Glenn spun around, but instead of dropping it, he pressed the trigger on his automatic weapon. Unknown to him it was set on full auto. The Mexican gunman dove behind a boulder, as bullets splattered in the rocks and rattled through the trees. Glenn held the trigger until it quit. By the time the clip was empty the smoking barrel was pointed straight up in the air.

"You are out of ammo," the Mexican said as Glenn struggled with the clip. "Now, drop the gun and stand very still."

Glenn did as he was told. "Who are you?" he asked the gunmen.

"That doesn't matter," the man replied. He was holding a small Mac10 automatic machine pistol. Glenn had seen them in the movies but never in person. "You are a cowboy, no?" the gunmen asked. "You wear an old time cowboy pistol. Are you a fast draw, Cowboy? Just like Wild Bill Hitchcock in the old western movies?"

While he was taunting Glenn, the arrogant assassin made the mistake of lowering his Mac10 and placing it by his side, like he was going to draw it from a holster. "Okay, Cowboy, I'm going to count to three. Then we will see. . . ."

Before the arrogant Mexican ever said one, Glenn yanked his Colt and fired, hitting the startled assassin square in the chest. Glenn's second bullet hit right on top of the first, driving the already dead gunman backwards off the boulder and onto the ground.

"It was Hickok!" Glenn said, looking down at the fallen assassin, "Wild Bill Hickok!" He dove for cover as another bullet ricocheted off the rock at his feet. After seeing Glenn kill their companion, the snipers down below had taken a crack at him. Just as Glenn hit the dirt he heard four more quick shots from the direction of the snipers. When the shooting ended he managed to get another clip in the AK-47 and jacked in a live round, but before he could get to his feet, someone hit him in the back of the head and he went down.

"We'll use him as bait for the others," Flaco Flores said. "Let's get him back to Cruz before the big one gets back up here."

"What happened?" Cruz asked Flaco when they rode up to them. "Where are the others?"

"Dead," Flaco said, "This one and the longhaired hombre got them."

"I tried to tell you," Parnell said.

"Tell me what?" Cruz asked.

"You boy's may be good at drive-by shooting against unarmed innocent people in the city, but up here...you ain't so hot. I warned you, those cowboys are nobody to mess around with."

Enraged, Cruz pulled his Glock and pointed it at Parnell, "One more word from you and I will kill you myself."

"Don't," Cassidy said, "We'll never get out of here if you do."

"Those cowboys just got lucky this time," Cruz said. "From now on, we all stick together. The next time we fight, they will all die."

"What do you want to do with this one?" Flaco asked, pointing to Glenn.

"Bring him along," Cruz said, "We will make him tell us where the others are."

"They should be right over this next ridge," Parnell said. "At first light, we'll catch 'em down there and get this over with."

"Somebody's coming," Colt said when he heard horses up above.

"Come on," Clark said, heading into the timber. When they were safely hidden, Colt spotted Reno coming down the slope, leading Glenn's horse. Fearing the worst, Colt stood up and whistled.

"Get on," Reno said when he got to them, "We got to get out of here. They're right over the ridgeline." Colt got up on Glenn's horse and Clark got on behind him.

"Where's Glenn?" Colt asked.

"I think they got him." Reno said over his shoulder.

When they were back in the camp, Colt was anxious to know about Glenn. "Why do you think they have Glenn?"

"We were ambushed by a couple of them with a sniper rifle," Reno said. "I left Glenn up above and I went after them. I heard a bunch of shooting, but when I got back up there, Glenn was gone."

"Do you think they killed him?"

"I don't think so," Reno said. "I think Glenn got one of them, before they got him. They left their dead companion lying up there. I don't think they would have taken Glenn if he was dead. He'd be of no use to them."

"What are we going to do?" Clark asked.

"As soon as it's dark," Reno said, "We're going to get him back."

It was long after dark as Cruz and Cassidy sat dozing around the fire with the other gunmen. They were all worn out from the hard ride into the wilderness. Glenn was tied up and sitting on a log a little distance away from the fire. He had a big knot on his head and a raging headache. He was silently cussing himself for getting caught.

With three of Cruz's men dead, the assassins were down to just seven gunmen. "Where is Parnell?" Cruz asked, suddenly sitting up and looking around the fire."

"He's feeding the horses," Cassidy said, "but he's been gone for a while."

"Go and see," Cruz said to Flaco.

After several minutes went by the gunmen returned with startling news, "Parnell is gone!"

"Gone," Cruz repeated, "Gone where?"

"How the hell would I know?" Flaco said. "He's just gone. All of the horses are gone. I think the food is gone too."

"He left us alone up here," Cassidy exclaimed. Suddenly on his feet, he was near panic. "I don't...he couldn't...how will we get out of here? What will we eat?" Unseen by the gunmen, Glenn was smiling to himself at edge of the fire.

Parnell was easing the pack string along a dark trail about a mile below them. He couldn't understand what they were saying, but he could clearly hear their excited voices as they debated their future. "No Mexican son-of-a-bitch is going to threaten me and get away with it," he said to his horse. Parnell had no intention of taking the blame for murdering the rangers. He planned to get to the ranger station at Squaw Lake, tell them what was going on and explain that he had no part in it.

"Shut up, you fool," Cruz said to Cassidy. "I have a satellite phone right here in my bag. When the gringos are all dead, I'll call Juan Carlos and have a chopper pick us up. With any luck, we'll be out of here tomorrow."

Out in the darkness, as Cruz and Cassidy were arguing, Reno took hold of Colt's sleeve and pointed. Colt nodded, indicating that he saw Glenn's silhouette in the firelight. Reno cupped his hand to Colt's ear and whispered. "Ease you way up there and drag him down behind that log."

"What are you going to do?" Colt whispered.

"I'm going around the other side. Don't wait on me. As soon as you're in position, get Glenn out of the line of fire."

"What about me?" Clark asked.

"Take Colt's rifle and get down a little farther, when you can get a line on them without hitting Glenn, stay there. Use a tree for a rest, if the shooting starts, pick one out and kill him. Just watch out for me."

"Kill him," Clark said, "Without giving them a chance to give up?"

"If you got a problem with that, you're no good to me," Reno said.

"No...no," Clark said, "I'm good."

"What was that?" Flaco asked, staring out into the darkness.

"I didn't hear anything," Cruz said, "You're getting as bad as this coward here."

"No," Flaco said, "Something is out there."

The gunmen were all concentrating on the soft sound out in front of them, when Glenn suddenly went ass over appetite into the darkness beyond the log. "What the. . . ." he tried to say as Colt dragged him down and clamped his hand over Glenn's mouth, "Shut up, Reno's out there."

"Untie my hands," Glenn whispered, "Where's my gun?"

"Where is the cowboy?" Flaco asked, suddenly turning back to the fire. The others jumped to their feet and started for the log.

"That's far enough," a strong voice said from the darkness. Cruz was standing with his men when Reno walked into the light of the fire. "Where did you come from?" Cruz asked.

"I wouldn't worry about that."

"Then why are you. . . ."

"I'm here to kill you." Reno said, "All of you." Cassidy's face went pale when he heard that.

"Why would you want to kill me?" Cruz asked, "You look like a bandito, you are one of us."

"I am not one of you. You are cowards and murderers."

"I'm sorry you feel that way, but killing me may not be so easy for one man alone."

"He ain't alone," Colt said from the darkness.

"I see," Cruz said, still watching Reno, "There are two of you, but there is seven of us. Suppose, just for a moment, while you are killing me, Flaco over there will be killing you?"

"Flaco won't kill me," Reno said pushing his hat back and letting it fall between his shoulders, "But that won't keep me from killing all of you."

"Flaco!" Cruz blurted out and went for his gun. Before Flaco or any of the others could move, Reno pulled the 870 from under his coat and began firing. Flaco never got off the first round. He was killed instantly by a 30-06 bullet ripping through his chest. The buckshot from Reno was shredding the gunmen as he worked the pump and yanked the trigger. Cassidy was on the ground curled up in a ball holding his head as the gunmen fell around him.

Colt killed one of the gunmen and Glenn accounted for one more. When the 870 went dry, Reno dropped it and pulled his Berettas. It wasn't necessary, the battle was over and the assassins were all dead.

As soon as the gunfire ended, Glenn, Colt, and Clark rushed to the fire. There among the scattered bodies, they saw Cassidy lying limp on the ground. He wasn't hit. He had fainted during the heat of battle. "We'll take this one back for the authorities," Reno said after finally smacking Cassidy enough to bring him around. "He can tell them who put them up to this."

"I don't know what you're talking about," Cassidy mumbled.

"If that's true, then you'll die right here," Reno said, feeding fresh rounds into his shotgun, "We'd have no reason to spare your life."

"All right," Cassidy said, "I'll tell them, but there are powerful people involved in this. You men are all marked after this. You won't live more than twenty-four hours after we get back."

"You're a lot like your great-grandfather," Reno said.

"My great-grandfather was a hero."

"Wilbur Cassidy was a gutless, murdering coward. He died on his knees, begging for his life, just like you're doing now."

"How would you know that?"

"I just know."

"I don't believe it."

"What you believe matters little to me," Reno said, "and it doesn't change the truth."

By first light the next morning, they were loaded and ready to go. Cassidy was up on one of the pack mules. "Which way?" Colt asked as Clark checked his GPS unit.

"I'm...not sure," Clark said, tapping on the small screen, "I ah...the damn thing is dead and I ah...forgot to bring any batteries. Any of you have a compass?"

"Would you know what to do with it if we did?" Colt asked.

"Put that thing away," Reno said, "We're going out at Squaw Lake."

"Do you know how to get there?" Clark asked.

"I believe I do," Reno said turning his horse. The others fell in line and followed him down the ridge.

It was late the next afternoon when they met five men on horseback coming up the trail they were on. The men seemed uneasy as they rode up on Reno. The one in front was wearing a forest service uniform and a gun. The others were in camouflage and armed to the teeth. The patch on their shoulders indicated they were U.S. Marshals. Parnell was with them. "Who are you men?" the ranger asked.

"Colt Hobbs from Reno," Colt said riding to the front. "We've been up at the crash site where my dad died."

"These are the men those hired killers were after," Parnell said, "That's Cassidy on the mule."

"Mr. Cassidy," one of the marshals said, "You're under arrest."

"What for?" Cassidy asked.

"You have the right to remain silent. . . ." the others waited until Cassidy had been informed of his rights. When he was finished, the marshal dragged Cassidy off the mule and handcuffed him.

"Where are Ranger Cooper and his intern?" the ranger asked.

"They wouldn't know anything about that," Parnell said before Colt could answer.

"Bill Curry," the first Marshal said holding his hand out to Colt.

"Good to meet you," Colt said shaking his hand.

"What about Cruz Portillo?" Marshal Curry asked.

"I don't know any of their names," Colt said, "But if he was with those hired killers, he's dead, along with all the others. They tried to kill us to keep us from the crash site. Kidnapped Glenn over there, planned to kill him too. We were forced to defend ourselves in the attempt to get him back."

"Are their bodies near the site?"

"Yes sir," Colt said, "Just above it. There's three more on the big rocky bluff to the south."

"You men are free to go for now," Curry said, "Parnell has made it pretty clear what was going on up there. I'm sure there will be plenty of questions later."

"What about Cassidy?" Colt asked.

"We'll take care of Mr. Cassidy," Curry said, "But I want to know one thing."

"What's that?" Colt said.

"How did the four of you manage to kill a dozen heavily armed professional killers and not one of you got hurt?"

"Well, hell," Glenn said with a big grin, "We're cowboys."

Chapter Thirteen: The Reckoning

It was just after breakfast a week later, when Gordon was sitting on the front porch reading a copy of the latest Gazette-Journal. "You boys seen the paper?" he asked as Reno and Colt joined him.

"Can't say that I have," Colt replied.

"Cassidy is singing his head off over in California. They've granted Parnell immunity for his testimony. They haven't found the guy who brought Teddy down, but they know who he is and they're closing in on him. With the addition of all the evidence you boys brought back, things are pretty much in the toilet for the damn wind power people."

"That's good news," Reno said.

"What about Reed Henry?" Colt asked.

"They've arrested him for conspiracy, murder, money laundering, and half-a-dozen other things," Gordon said, "He's in federal custody in Sacramento, along with Juan Carlos the banker, and Don Chow the Chinese wind turbine guy. The whole damn bunch is in the jail house over there."

"That's not all," Charley said, joining them on the porch, "It seems when things started falling apart, it really went wrong for the wind power people. They had almost thirty million dollars worth of turbines sitting on the dock in San Diego. The very same ones that they wanted to put on our ranch. Three nights ago all of them were destroyed in a horrendous fire. The authorities think it was caused by a leaking fuel storage tank nearby, but they're not sure what set it off."

"I guess we won't be seeing any of those things on the ridges around here anytime soon," Colt said.

"I think Dad would be proud of all of you," Charley said.

Next morning Reno walked into Charley's clinic. "Can I help you, Sir," she asked when she saw him come in.

"I thought it might be nice to see where you work," he said.

"It's a little quiet right now, I'm afraid."

"Why is that?" Reno asked.

"It's the economy. A lot of ranchers are doing their own doctoring or just putting it off all together. With these ridiculous fuel prices, things are tough for everybody that's trying to ranch."

"How are things here?"

"This is just between you and me," she said. "Things are not too good. Gordon was getting a little careless about some financial things and Colt, well you know Colt. Dad and I have been taking care of the finances around here for the last two years. Now with him gone, it's all fallen on my shoulders."

"Even though this ranch has been in our family for years, there are still debts to pay. Some years back when Gordon was healthy, he would make a couple hundred grand in a year, sometimes more. I'm afraid that hasn't happened lately.

"I could probably make more money if I specialized in equine medicine. I would have to live in an area where there was a big interest in high dollar horses, but I love this ranch. I don't want to be anywhere else. I figure as long as I can squeeze out a living here, I'm staying.

"It's no secret that most cattle ranchers borrow money every year to operate on and pay it back after they ship the feeder calves in the fall. We do that just like everybody else, only the last few years have been extremely bad. We have carried some debt over each year until it's close to a quarter-million dollars."

"That's a lot of money," he said, "even today."

"It is, but it's even worse than that. A new bank holding company has managed to get control of our loan. They want it paid right away. Now, with Shock Waves dead, there's no way to do that without liquidating most of our cattle or selling off some of the land. Or. . . ."

"Or what?"

"Before you all stopped Cassidy and those wind power people, I was convinced they were behind this. If we had let them put those turbines on the ranch, we would have had the money. Now, I just don't know."

"I think I can help," Reno said, "If you'll let me."

"I'm not going to borrow money from you."

"That's good," he said, "because I don't have any money."

"Then how do you propose to help?"

"Do you have time to take a ride?"

"I'm pretty busy," she said looking around the empty room, "but I suppose I can make time for you. Where are we going?"

"You'll see," he said heading for the door, "I'll be right back."

Reno ran to the barn and put a bridle on his horse. He rode bareback to the clinic and helped Charley up behind him. "Which way is the old house from here?"

"Down through that draw," Charley said, pointing to the south, "About a quarter of a mile."

After riding down to the ruins of the original house, Reno slid off and helped Charley down. The only thing left was the rock foundation and a few rotten timbers. "The house is gone," he said looking around, "but the land hasn't changed."

"How would you know that?"

"I...ah...I heard Gordon describe it."

"Reno," she said, "I know this is going to sound like I've lost my mind, but. . . ."

"But what," he asked.

"My Aunt Martha described the Reno Kid pretty well in her diary."

"What's that to do with me?"

"Everything she wrote about him...the similarities, it's as if she was writing it about you, the amulet you wear, the scar on your chest, your looks, the way you...everything, but that's impossible, right? Please tell me what to believe."

"You're right, it is impossible."

"That didn't tell me what. . . ."

Reno walked away before she could finish. Charley followed him trying to figure out what he seemed to be looking for. He led her up the side of a steep hill and over into a little hollow. There was a pile of boulders there and some tailings, where some old time prospector must have been digging.

Reno was on his knees as he began pulling at the rocks. It was only a moment until he uncovered a small hollow under the boulder. Reaching in, he withdrew a rotted burlap bundle. Inside was a small metal box. "Is that made of silver? It looks ancient," Charley said, going down on her knees beside him. "How did you know. . . .?"

"Don't ask," he said. "Just keep telling yourself this is impossible." After blowing away the dust and prying open the tarnished lid, Reno removed a small leather pouch. Opening it up, he checked the contents and handed it to Charley.

"What are these?" She asked pouring them out in her palm, "Oh my, they're...they can't be."

"Diamonds," Reno said, "Uncut, but they're diamonds."

"Some of these must be three or four carats."

"I wouldn't know about that."

"But how did you? Where did they come from? How long have they been here? Are they yours?"

"They were, but now they're yours. I really have no use for them."

"But this box, these stones, they're worth a fortune."

"I hope so, that'll help solve your problem."

"Reno, I can't...how will I do this?" Charley asked. "How do I sell them? Who'll buy them?"

"Take them to the Chin Ho Diamond Wholesalers in San Francisco. Be sure and take the silver box. It was hand-made by the original Chin Ho. Tell them these stones were found by Chin Ho and his good friend near Cherokee, California back around, 1855."

"His good friend," she said, "1855, that can't be. What was this good friend's name?"

"That's right," he said, without answering her question, "It may be hard to believe, but tell them anyway. When they see the craftsmanship that went into this box and the signature inside, they will believe you, trust me."

"How can I ever. . . ." Before she could finish, Charley threw her arms around him and pushed him to the ground. She began kissing him and pulling at his clothes. The afternoon sun was hot on their bodies as they made love right there in the sagebrush.

After an hour or so, they were lying on the ground next to each other. Charley raised herself up on one elbow and turned to him. "Is this where you made love to Aunt Martha?"

"I don't know what you're talking about."

"Yes, you do," she said, "I know it seems nearly impossible, but I believe it with all my heart."

"Trust me, you don't want your heart involved in this," he said.

"I know, I've read all about it. You had to leave Martha to save her life, but you don't have to leave me. The threat to me is gone now. You can stay here, with me. I...I love you, Augustus. I don't want you to go...please don't leave me."

"It may not be up to me," he said, ignoring the fact that she had just used his real name.

"Yes, it is. Things are going to be just fine around here now. You're staying. Mark my words, you can be happy here."

"Charley, I haven't been happy. . . ."

"No," she said holding up her hand. "This is a great day and I'm not going to let you spoil it."

Charley was in a really care-free mood as she flitted around the house that evening. They were just sitting down to supper when the telephone rang. Charley answered it, "Hello...yes this is Charley...Hi Posey. Hold on, I'm going to put you on speakerphone. Okay, go ahead."

"Is Rosebud there?" Posey asked.

"I'm here," Glenn said, "What's up?"

"I found out who poisoned Shock Waves."

"Who?"

"Bubba Bramlett."

"The whiskey soaked rodeo clown?"

"The very same."

"How did you find out?" Charley asked.

"The dumb-ass was sitting in the Spur last night buying drinks for everybody. After he was about three-sheets-in-the-wind, I asked him about his sudden wealth. He was trying to be clever, said he got hit by a Shock Wave."

"Did he tell you he did it for sure?" Glenn said.

"Not until I met him at his pickup a little later," Posey said, "I just kept beating the hell out of him until he admitted it. Claimed a man from Reno...Cassidy, I think his name was, paid him to do it. Bubba looked up cattle poisons on the internet and found out he could use a common pesticide. There was plenty of that around his daddy's ranch, and Bubba knows just enough about cattle to make your bull drink it."

"Where is he now?" Colt asked.

"In the hospital…will be for a spell."

"Let me think about this and we'll get back to you," Charley said.

"I'll be waiting," Posey said, "If you want, Ms. Charley, I'll kill him for you. I'll bury his worthless ass out in the desert, doubt if anybody would even look for him."

"That won't be necessary Posey, but I appreciate the offer."

"So long Rosebud, see you down the line."

"So long, Posey," Glenn said as Charley hung up the receiver.

"Should we get the law involved?" Charley asked turning to Gordon.

"Cassidy's already in jail," Gordon said, "And after all is said and done, they won't send Bubba to jail for killing a bull."

"We could sue him," Colt said.

"Bubba don't have two nickels to rub together," Glenn said.

"What about his daddy?" Colt asked.

"His daddy didn't have anything to do with this," Gordon said, "Why would we sue him?"

"I suppose the only thing to do is forget it," Charley said.

"I say, you tell Posey to kill him," Reno said, "Or we go up there and do it ourselves."

"That's not funny," Charley said.

"It wasn't meant to be funny."

"Enough about Bubba Bramlett, let's eat," Charley said, ending the conversation.

That same evening in Sacramento, a deputy U.S. marshal was signing some paper work and taking custody of several prisoners. "Where are you taking these men at this time in the evening?" the guard asked.

"No offense," the marshal said to the officer, "but this is U.S. Government business. I'm not at liberty to say."

"It just seems that you have a small security detail to be handling so many high profile prisoners."

"There are more waiting outside," the marshal said, "Could you just get them for me."

"Did they give you any trouble?" Marshal Curry asked the deputy when he was outside.

"No, it went just like you said."

"Good job," Curry said, "Get them in the van and let's get out of here."

"Where are you taking us?" Reed Henry demanded, as he was being loaded in the van.

"Shut up and get in," Curry said.

"You can't talk to me like that, I'm a U.S. Senator."

"You were a U.S. Senator," Curry said shoving Henry through the door, "Now get in." Cassidy, Chow, and Carlos were right behind him.

The van left the jail and proceeded to the airport. The driver went through a remote unguarded gate and pulled up next to a small unmarked corporate jet. "Get them in the plane," Curry said to the three marshals that were with him.

The marshals from Curry's security detail escorted the prisoners to the door of the jet and turned them over to two more uniformed marshals. Curry was the last one to board. Just before the hatch was closed, Curry told the security detail to take the van back to the office.

"Where are we going?" Juan Carlos asked as the jet began to taxi.

"Rollo wants to talk to you four," Curry said, "Something about fifty million dollars of his money being missing."

"Now hold on," Henry said, "You can't kidnap us."

"Nobody said anything about kidnapping you," Curry said, "You're free. In just a few hours we'll be in Mexico." While he was talking, Curry pulled a small transmitter from his front pocket and pulled the antenna up. He was looking out the window as the jet became airborne. Holding the transmitter to the Plexiglas, Curry pressed the button. Far below, a huge fireball erupted on the freeway.

"You can't get away with this," Cassidy said, "The authorities will be after you before we ever get to Mexico."

"All the authorities know is that you're no longer in Sacramento. They have no clue where you are now, and they never will."

"What about those marshals that brought us here?" Cassidy said.

"Shut up stupid," Henry said, "Who do you think the detonator was for?"

It was midnight when the jet touched down in Sonora. There were two vans waiting for them at a small hanger just off the taxiway. After unloading his prisoners, Curry told them goodbye. "I have to get back," he said, "These gentlemen will take you the rest of the way."

"Where are we going?" Henry asked.

"A lovely place," Curry said, "But I don't think you're going to enjoy it." As the vans departed, the jet was quickly refueled and lifted off a short time later.

Chapter Fourteen: Return of the Phantom Warriors

The vans traveled south for an hour before turning off the highway. After leaving the pavement, they traveled another three miles on a narrow gravel road. At the end of the gravel, they passed through a guarded gate and entered an adobe walled compound.

"Lock them up," one of the van drivers said to the armed men waiting inside the compound.

The heavily armed guards escorted the four prisoners to a small windowless building and locked them in. One guard remained behind to watch the door. "Find the lights," Cassidy said when they were inside, "I can't see a thing."

Chow managed to find a switch and flipped it up. The barren little room was illuminated by a single bare bulb suspended from the ceiling. There were four dirty mattresses scattered around on the concrete floor and a bucket in the corner. The smell coming from it, made it plain what it was there for.

At noon the next day, the prisoners were summoned to appear in front of the mysterious and reclusive Rollo. They were led to a spacious veranda looking out over miles of empty country. Armando Rollo was sitting at a table spread with fresh flowers and fruit. A young oriental girl was sitting across the table from him. Eduardo Villa, a huge Mexican enforcer, stood vigil behind the drug king. Eduardo was one of Rollo's well trained and heavily armed personal body guards.

"Gentleman," Rollo said, "I hope you weren't too uncomfortable last night."

"This is an outrage!" Henry shouted, "Put me in touch with the consulate right now."

"Senator Henry," Rollo warned, "It would be in your best interest to remain silent. You have no friends or political power here."

"Shut up Reed," Juan Carlos said, "Or I'll kill you myself."

"Juan Carlos and Don Chow, I know," Rollo said. "Who is this man?" he asked pointing to Cassidy.

"Will Cassidy, Nevada Alternate Energy," Cassidy said.

"What is your part in this?"

"I was securing the leases for the turbines."

"I see," Rollo said. "Well Gentlemen, I suppose you are wondering what you are doing here. I will tell you. I have lost over fifty million U.S. dollars because of your blunder."

"Fifty million," Henry repeated, "That can't be right. It was nowhere near that much."

"Most of the money is tied up in those turbines in San Diego," Carlos said, "It can easily be recovered."

"I'm afraid you are wrong," Rollo said. "Tell him, Chow."

"My lawyer informed me those turbines were deliberately destroyed two nights ago," Chow said, "They are a total loss."

"You can't hold us responsible for that," Henry said.

"Tell them the rest," Rollo said to Chow.

"There was another product stored in those turbines."

"Another product," Henry said, "What other product?"

"Cocaine," Rollo said, "More than three million dollars in each one."

"We were smuggling drugs?" Henry asked.

"It was a perfect plan," Rollo said, "The drugs traveled by freighter from Mexico to China. Chow's men concealed them in the turbines and shipped them to America. The erection contractors were financed by our coalition. They were to take delivery of the turbines, remove the drugs and get them to my distributors. It all fell apart when you fools couldn't get the permits to erect them."

"What do you want us to do about that now?" Juan Carlos asked.

"I want my money back," Rollo said.

"Where are we going to get fifty million dollars?" Henry asked.

"That is something you must decide in the next few minutes," Rollo said. "I am not a patient man."

"My company will pay for my share," Chow said, "Just get word to them and I'm sure we can work this out."

"Very well," Rollo said. "And you Juan Carlos?"

"Most of the money in my bank is yours, Armando. I was only acting at your request. You know I don't have that kind of money."

"Very well my old friend," Rollo said after a moment of thought, "What you say is true. You were only doing what you were told. I forgive you."

"Thank you, Armando. God bless you."

"I hope you will forgive me," Rollo said.

Juan Carlos was puzzled, "Forgive you?"

"For your wife."

"My wife."

"I was very angry at first, perhaps I acted in haste. I am sorry."

"I…I forgive you."

"Thank you, my dear friend and God bless you. Release, Juan Carlos," Rollo said to Eduardo, "Have someone show him to a room where he can shower and give him something to eat. He can go back to Mexico City in the morning."

"Now for you, Mr. Cassidy, how do you plan to repay me?"

"I'm just a public servant," Cassidy claimed, "I have no money."

"Will Nevada pay to get you back?"

"No, at least I don't think so."

"That is too bad," Rollo said, motioning to Eduardo.

"No, wait!" Cassidy begged, "You can't do this!" Cassidy managed to avoid Eduardo's grasp and began to run across the veranda. Eduardo pulled a large semi-auto pistol from under his coat, stepped around the table and fired three shots into Cassidy's back. The impact of the bullets drove Cassidy over the short veranda wall. His lifeless body landed with a thud in the dirt of the compound below.

"And now, Senator, we come to you."

"I'm worth plenty," Henry said, seemingly unshaken by Cassidy's murder, "My influence goes to very highest level in the federal government."

"The very highest," Rollo said, "Do you mean. . . ."

"The very highest," Henry repeated. "I know what they have planned for America and they will pay plenty to keep me quiet about it."

"But you are little more than a prisoner in America."

189

"Hardly," Henry said, "There was a pardon in the works if I was ever convicted. I wasn't going to jail."

"How do you propose we get the money?"

"Get me in front of a video camera. I'll tell you everything I know. Download a copy to my personal secretary. Tell her to forward it to Alpha. Put an attachment in with the video. Tell Alpha you're going to send a copy to every conservative media outlet in the free world. I'm pretty sure you can name your own price."

"All right," Rollo said, "We'll try that. Take him to the media room," he said to the guards.

It was two days later when Rollo summoned Henry and Chow to the veranda. "Mr. Chow," he said, "Far East has agreed to reimburse me for the turbines and the other product that was lost in California. They see a bright future for our partnership and they want to continue."

"I knew they would want me back," Chow said, "When do I leave?"

"They see a future with me, not you."

"What do you mean?"

"Being a wanted felon, you're worthless to them in the U.S. and they don't need you back in China. They said you would understand." Rollo motioned for Eduardo to take Chow away.

"What are you going to do with him?" Henry asked.

"You don't want to know."

"What about me?"

Rollo held up his hand for silence until Chow was gone. "You, my friend, are a very important man."

"I told you," Henry said.

"They will pay, but only part of it will be in cash. They can't hide that much money in such a short time frame. The rest of my money will be repaid in confiscated weapons and National Guard ammunition."

"Is that all right with you?"

"Of course," Rollo said, "I told them I would credit fifty cents on the dollar for the weapons and munitions. There is a huge market for that sort of thing both here and in Africa."

"How long?"

"I don't know, but you will be my guest until they deliver the goods."

Just after lunch the next day, Reno went to the barn to feed his horse. Walking through the door he was confronted by three familiar faces. "We meet again, little brother," Theseus said.

"Theseus, Orpheus," Reno said, "It is good to finally see you again. It has been a long time. Where have you been?"

"San Diego," Theseus said.

"It is time to go," Perseus said.

"The battle seems to be over," Reno said.

"Only the first," Perseus said, "You have done well, but a powerful evil still exists in the land of Chimalpopoca."

"When do we leave?" Reno asked.

"We must go now," Perseus said, "A great battle awaits us."

"Saddle your Dire, Augustus," Orpheus said, "We ride."

The four of them were mounted and headed south as darkness surrounded them. "It is a good day," Theseus said as they rode.

"Why is that?" Augustus asked.

"After all these long centuries, the four of us are finally together, Perseus, Theseus, Orpheus, and Augustus."

Charley had just set dinner on the table when Glenn and Colt came in to join the rest of the family. "Me and Colt are going to the Nugget tonight," Glenn said to Charley, "You want to go?"

"Is Reno going?" Charley asked.

"I haven't asked him," Glenn said.

"Where is he anyway?" Charley asked.

"I don't rightly know," Glenn said, "His pickup is out there, but his horse is gone."

"Gone," Charley repeated, jumping to her feet, "No...no...no," she kept saying all the way out the door.

The next morning, two loaded semi's pulled into Rollo's compound just as an unmarked Huey helicopter appeared over head. The chopper sat down in a wide spot at the north end of the compound. The pilot and the occupants remained inside while the dust settled and the blades spun down.

Rollo's men opened the trailers and carefully inspected the contents. After nearly an hour, they were satisfied with the cargo. One of them stepped out into the courtyard and signaled up to the veranda. "It is time for you to go," Rollo said to Reed Henry."

The truck drivers were making their way to the chopper as Henry came down from the veranda. "Goodbye my friend!" Rollo shouted from the balcony, "I will see you soon!"

"Not likely, you pompous son-of-a-bitch," Henry mumbled to himself, all the while smiling and waving to Rollo.

The chopper blades began to turn up as Henry climbed aboard. Just before it lifted off, two quick shots were heard from the interior and the bodies of the truck drivers were dumped out on the ground. In less than a minute, Reed Henry and the unseen occupants of the chopper were gone.

Late that evening, Rollo, one of his lieutenants, and Eduardo were sitting on the veranda watching the sun go down. "The cash is safely stored away," the lieutenant said.

"And the weapons?" Rollo asked.

"They are still in the trucks. I have brokered a deal with the Somalia's for a big part of the shipment. We will start for the coast tomorrow."

"What kind of deal did you make?"

"You will be pleased," the lieutenant said handing Rollo a stack of computer printouts. "Your fifty million dollars had turned into nearly one hundred and twenty. . . ."

"What is that?" Rollo asked as a smoky shadow swept across the veranda, scattering papers from the table as it went.

"I don't. . . ." A blaring horn began to sound from the security tower as another huge shadow swept through the compound below. "Something has tripped a sensor in the hills!" the lieutenant shouted.

"The Americans!" Rollo replied.

"I don't know. . . ."

"Go and find out!"

As soon as the lieutenant got to his feet, he spotted four huge dark shadows approaching from the north. "What is that?" he asked.

Rollo was on his feet as the lieutenant began yelling into a walkie-talkie. Armed men began pouring out of the house as a sound like running horses pervaded the compound. Rollo grew pale when he spotted the huge beasts coming across the hills toward his fortress. "What in God's name is that?" he asked.

"I don't know," Eduardo said, "I think…we need to go." The lieutenant hurried away to join his men in the courtyard.

The huge dark beasts swept over the wall and stopped inside the compound. The men down below were terror stricken as the dark phantoms astride the beasts began to dismount. Part of the guards dropped their weapons and fled. The others began spraying automatic rifle fire into the approaching phantoms.

Rollo thought he was in the middle of a nightmare. The once all powerful drug king was witnessing his elite security force being overwhelmed right in front of his eyes. The dark phantom warriors seemed immune to the swarm of bullets in the air. He stood transfixed by terror as the phantoms unsheathed long shining swords and began slaughtering every man in the compound.

Blood was standing in pools on the ground and running down the adobe walls, as the merciless phantoms went about their terrible work. Finally giving in to Eduardo's urging, Rollo followed the big man down the dark steps that led to his reinforced underground safe room.

Arriving at the sanctuary entrance in a growing panic, Eduardo entered the wrong access code. The key pad beside the massive locking mechanism was flashing red as Eduardo frantically tried again.

"Let me do it, you fool!" Rollo shouted, pushing Eduardo out of the way. Huge beads of sweat were dripping down the drug king's face. With his heart ready to explode and his breath coming in gasps, he realized heavy footsteps were coming down the stairs from the compound.

"Hurry, Rollo, hurry!" Eduardo begged, "They are coming!"

Finally gaining access to the room, Eduardo closed the door behind them and activated the electric locks. Once safely inside the sanctuary,

Rollo found several of his concubines and house servants were already there huddled together in the corner. The once all powerful drug king grabbed a satellite phone and began screaming for help as some unseen being began to savagely pound on the heavy stainless steel door.

The pounding was deafening inside the tiny room. With his nerves shattered, Rollo dropped the phone and watched in horror as the door began to buckle. The pounding continued until the supposedly impenetrable door fell into the room and a tall dark phantom stepped through the dust.

Eduardo pulled his pistol, but instead of firing at the phantom, he placed the muzzle against his own temple and pulled the trigger. The bullet emerging from his skull splattered blood on the hysterical women as the big Mexican's body fell limp to the floor.

The towering dark phantom pushed his long black hair out of his face, revealing glowing yellow eyes with narrow black pupils. The once merciless drug lord fell to his knees and clasped his hands as those terrible cruel eyes focused on him. In answer to Rollo's plea for mercy, the dark phantom raised his face to the ceiling and uttered a resounding thunderous roar. A shining sword suddenly appeared over the phantom's head and Rollo, yearning for a swift death and an end to this nightmare, threw himself down at the phantom's feet.

The safe room was silent after only a moment. The walls were covered in blood as the phantom emerged through the opening and went to rejoin the battle outside.

By the time darkness had descended on the compound, all was silent. The buildings were in flames and everyone who dwelt there was dead. Explosions ripped through the darkness as loads of weapons, ammunition, cash, and drugs were consumed in the flames. The Dires and their terrible vengeful riders were gone.

It was right after breakfast two days later when Gordon shouted from the living room, "Something's going on, you all better come here. I think they may be going to say something about the missing prisoners." Colt, Glenn, and Charley joined him as regular programming was interrupted by a bulletin from the White House. The press room was filled with reporters when the spokesman walked to the podium. Reed Henry was right behind him.

"Well I'll be a. . . ." Gordon started to say.

"Wait," Charley said, "I want to hear this."

"Thank you for coming," the spokesman said to the group assembled in the room. "I'm here to tell you that a major victory has been won in the President's war on drugs. Reed Henry, the senior Senator from Nevada, has been working with the DEA in an undercover sting operation against a large, internationally financed, drug smuggling cartel. It was reported in the news recently that he had been arrested along with several international financiers in California.

"I'm happy to say, that little ruse worked to perfection and Senator Henry was able to infiltrate the smugglers ranks. Upon his narrow, and I might add, harrowing escape, he revealed to us where the drugs and illegal weapons were located and who was running the operation. This man is a true American hero, ladies and gentleman."

"What about the smugglers?" one of the reporters asked. "Who are they, what's going to happen to them?"

"Most of those details are still classified," the spokesman said with an all knowing smile, "But I can tell you the latest satellite images confirm their stronghold has been totally destroyed. Of course, I can't really reveal where that is or who destroyed it." A quiet murmur of laughter went through the room when he said that. "This should reconfirm to all of you, this President will use every tool at his disposal to eliminate these drug dealers and the harm they do to America. The President will have some remarks a little later today, but for now I give you a great American, Senator Reed Henry."

Gordon hit the remote before Henry got to the microphone. "Can you believe that?" Colt asked.

"That man is a thief and a murderer," Charley said, "Now the whole country thinks he's a hero."

"Unfortunately," Gordon said, "If they see it on TV, most of the people in this country will believe anything."

"Do you think Reno had something to do with destroying that compound?" Charley asked.

"I'd bet my hat on it," Gordon said, "That's why he had to leave. It's just too bad he missed Reed Henry."

"Do you think we'll ever see him again?" Colt asked.

"Trouble will come back to this valley," Gordon said. "It may not be in my lifetime, but maybe you'll see him again."

"Do you really believe Reno is the original Reno Kid?" Colt asked.

"Why hell yeah, he is," Glenn said, before Gordon could answer. "I knew it all along. This is the west. It's big country and legends live here. I'm proud to say the Reno Kid is a friend of mine and I ain't scared to tell anybody that wants to listen."

"I would never say it outside this room," Charley said, "but I know for a fact, the Reno we knew and the Reno Kid from Aunt Martha's diary are one in the same."

"How can you be sure?" Colt asked. "I mean, I miss him and all. It ain't the same around here without him, but Reno being the Reno Kid, I don't know, it's almost too much to believe."

"There are a dozen reasons why I know, but I can't talk about them right now. We'll just have to wait and...hope. . . ." Charley paused for a moment to dab at the tear in her eye and regain her composure. "I know in my heart he'll come back. You just wait and see."

The End. . . . Not Likely!

CPSIA information can be obtained at www.ICGtesting.com
Printed in the USA
LVOW100549071111

253819LV00003B/1/P

9 781614 345084